American Fantastic

Proudly Presents

Delusions of Grandeur

Stories and Poems

by John Beechem

Delusions of Grandeur
First Edition April 2016
ISBN: 978-0692644492
Published by American Fantastic
AmericanFantastic.com

These stories and poems come from the imagination of a human being. They are not literal truth. They are the culmination of countless human experiences, too many to list here. Elements inspired by the author's own life have been cloaked by the glamour of fiction.

American Fantastic advocates for the liberated exchange of information and ideas, including a free and open internet.

We encourage our audience to support artists and writers any way they can. Those fortunate enough to have the means may pay for this book with local currency.

If poor circumstances or unjust economic conditions prevent you from being able to afford this book, please speak to the author or e-mail americanfantastic@gmail.com. Free and discount books are available to schools, libraries, prisons and those living in need.

For my dad, Tom Beechem,

who helped keep my imagination well fed.

TABLE OF CONTENTS

PART I

DOORS OF PERCEPTION

If the doors of perception were cleansed everything would appear to man as it is, infinite.

-William Blake

I tell you this, man, I tell you this. I don't know what's gonna happen, man, but I wanna have my kicks before the whole shit house goes up in flames.

-Jim Morrison

DELUSIONS OF GRANDEUR

At the last possible moment of endurance, Paul blew a cloud of smoke from his mouth. A wracking cough erupted from his throat as the bathroom filled with a sweet-smelling haze. He put his pipe on the rim of the sink, and grabbed his toothbrush and toothpaste, rapidly brushing away the taste and smell of the smoke while he fulfilled the demands of his meticulous morning hygiene routine.

Not that he had had much of a morning lately; at least, not the waking up part. He had become consumed by a symphonic blur of mental and spiritual energy, wrapped up in a kind of charged trance--a blend of rapid thought, obsessive focus, and revolutionary philosophizing. Paul knew about this tendency in those who were bi-polar, or "suffered from manic-depression" in the classic parlance. A kind of madness stirred one into a frenzy, and they would sometimes exorcize this excruciating ecstasy in a creative spree, forging works of genius, or at least profound quantities in a short time. Conversely, these same souls were sometimes crippled by darkness, wracked with a depressive despair. Usually, these black periods would pass on their own. Other times, their sufferers would end them prematurely, choosing to walk into the sea, wave a gun at a squad of police, fall off a bridge, or simply plunge a needle and thus numb the pain forever.

Lately, Paul had discovered how to harness his power in an attempt to ride the manic energy into the realm of cosmic discovery. But looking at himself in the mirror, his eyes watering with the hit he took—a quick remedy for boredom and excess energy, at least most of the time—he looked more like a burnout than a prophet. This week, nothing had been able to subdue the inferno inside his mind, including anti-histamines (labeled as sleep-aids), herbal tea, exercise, nor restless hours in bed. Not that he really needed much sleep anyway. Even two or three hours in this state kept him feeling heroic, like a highly evolved human being who had shed much of his need for rest. Or a prophet filled with a divine wind, having flashes of realization epiphany, or delusion if one felt a touch cynical.

After he spit into the sink and rinsed his mouth, Paul put his pipe away in his desk drawer and grabbed his backpack, swinging it around his shoulders. His fingers squeezed the buckle of his bike helmet, freeing it from the hoop of his right arm strap. He pulled the gleaming red and white bowl of plastic and foam over his head, and buckled it with a sharp click. His hands slapped his pockets a couple of times; once assured he had everything he needed for work (*wallet, phone, keys, mp3 player*), Paul opened his door, locked it behind him, and bounded down the steps into his apartment building's basement. Creeping down the stairs, a few dim rays of sun shining through the basement's windows led him to his bike locked around a narrow metal support column.

Paul unlocked it and rolled it alongside him, opened the basement door, and clumsily banged the bike through the door-frame before carrying it up half a dozen concrete steps. He set it down on a patch of grass in front of him, leaning it against a worn, wooden picnic table as he threaded the cords of his ear-buds through the straps of his helmet. Then his right hand gripped the center of the handlebar, and he led it down the slight incline of the apartment building's street-side yard. His body tensed with anticipation, eager to bolt into action, pedaling rapidly down the wide avenue near his home. It led to Harvest Morning Market, a local health food store where he worked. He only had about fifteen minutes before his morning shift started.

The rhythm of vehicles hummed past and eventually slowed enough to let Paul occupy a space in the lane closest to the sidewalk. A thudding revolutionary hip-hop M.C. blasted from his music player, providing the soundtrack for his ride. His slow acceleration relative to the cars and trucks zooming past built up to a feeling of liberation as the street began to decline. In his mania, the feeling of his muscles straining against the bike's pedals created a pulse of endorphins that fanned his flames even higher. Paul turned left at one of the intersections, placing him on Bardstown Road, a mixed assortment of hip shops, local restaurants, fast food chains and motorized traffic. He weaved his bicycle in and out of a parking lane, letting vehicles pass him, pointing an index finger in the direction of the lane he was about to enter, gripping the handlebar with his opposite hand.

As he made his way south, block by block, thoughts of self-divinity began to brew. He sensed an impending and irrevocable change: the spirit of revolution had touched him personally. He felt an emerging obsession with the idea that a raised middle and index finger, thumb touching the ring finger with the pinkie curled in, colloquially known as the peace sign was in fact a sign shared among those agents of positivity and natural preservation whose mission was to protect planet Earth. Obviously, such thoughts were an expression of madness, but a part of Paul's mind reflected on the realization that the central figures of most of the world's religions were accused of insanity (or would be in Paul's time).

The signals flashing through his neural receptors emerged as thoughts in his mind so rapidly, and were accepted as self-evident truth, that his experience began to mirror that of a psychedelic trip. The feeling coalesced that he and his co-workers at Harvest Morning, an assortment of young hipsters and older hippies, would soon be awakening an awareness that much of this world was an illusion about to be shattered. The idea came that all of them would soon emerge from a dream, and remember that they were superhuman, able to transform the world with their thoughts and actions. Paul felt as if he could step into this reality like a cicada emerging from its shell—fully formed and ready to confront anything.

He weaved his bike through the rear parking lot of an assortment of retailers that populated the shopping center, and leaned his bike against a wall. Paul pressed some buttons on the combination lock of the employee's entrance, and pulled his bike into the rear section of the store. It was a space with a concrete floor, racks of grocery overstock, and the entrance to a walk-in cooler and a walk-in freezer. The air-conditioned coolness of the store wrapped itself around him, and he led his bike to a space between two racks to lean it against one. He stopped his music and coiled the cords of his ear-buds around his device, placing it in his pocket. Paul shrugged his backpack off his shoulders and placed it on the bottom shelf of a rack for employees' possessions. The shape of the backpack imprinted itself on his shirt in a pattern of sweat that would turn cool and evaporate in the climate-controlled interior of the store.

Paul walked through the double swinging metal doors that led from the rear of the store into the retail area. A short hallway linked these two sections together. Inside his manager's office, he found one of his younger co-workers, Jesse, counting out money for that morning's till. Jesse looked up and smiled as Paul stood in the doorway.

"Hey, Paul, how's it going?" Jesse asked as he continued counting out the money.

Paul smiled slightly as he regarded Jesse in his seat. He closed the door of the office behind him and approached the desk.

"I'm good, man. Real good. Hey, it's about to start," Paul announced to him.

"What is?" Jesse asked.

"A revolution, I guess." Paul's thoughts began to telescope to perfect clarity. A number of movies came to his mind—ones of heroes suddenly answering a call to arms. He saw that he and his other co-workers at the store were these kind of heroes and would lead humankind past this critical juncture into a new age of joy and prosperity. At once, he recognized that he was the newest incarnation of Jesus Christ: a new messiah who would be cut down and usher in a new age of awareness and clarity. Those around him would be his disciples; his own wife, Mary Magdalene.

At the periphery of his consciousness, Paul realized that this was exactly what a crazy person would think. He knew that delusions of grandeur were a common symptom of mental illness, but at the same time, a new thought crept into his mind and acted as a counter-point. Jesus himself had delusions of grandeur. He declared himself the son of God. What greater delusion could there be? Yet he changed the world, irrevocably. Perhaps those who made the most impact were those who didn't listen to the voice inside their head that told them they were insane.

Paul envisioned he and his companions as part of a cycle of radical change. They were born into this world, over and over again, to inject a new age of revolution every time they came into existence. Inevitably, his incarnation was cut down, but others lived on to continue his work. Paul realized that he was a kind of avatar. His soul was continually reborn, but until now, there was no way that he could remember that that this was occurring. What was different about this cycle, he realized, was that he and his disciples would be able to record these realizations in crystal clarity, and no one would be able to tarnish or distort them as they had the words and deeds of his predecessors.

He leaned over the desk that Jesse was counting bills upon and began to speak in a conspiratorial tone. "Now listen. They're going to think I'm crazy. They'll come in here to take me away, and we're just going to...roll with it."

Jesse looked back at Paul slightly bemused. "Who is?" he asked grinning, arching his eyes to express his curiosity.

Paul ignored him as if this question didn't matter. Instead, he began describing in elaborate detail the vision and ideas he was having, slowly witnessing them develop in his mind as he articulated them aloud. Eventually, he became frustrated, because his words could not keep up with the pace of his thoughts, and his explanations became obscured in a fog of confusion for the both of them. Despite his best intentions, Paul's words fell flat. He and Jesse were not on the same trip, in a manner of speaking.   To punctuate this feeling of disconnect, Paul grabbed a pencil and flung it against the opposite wall.

Next, he opened the office's heavy wooden door and walked out into the Harvest Morning's retail area. He began to approach each of the few people in the store announce to them, one by one, "It's starting!" The bewildered customers noted him with incredulity, then continued shopping. Eventually, Paul circled back to the rear of the store and told Carolyn, an older, warm-hearted co-worker the same thing. Beaming with a smile, she asked in a confirming tone, "It is?" When Paul nodded and returned to the office to sit down in the seat Jesse no longer occupied, Carolyn calmly dialed 911 from the phone behind the customer service counter.

In the time between the phone call and the arrival of the police, Paul continued raving like a lunatic, albeit from inside the office. He was still hot and sweaty from his bike ride, and wanted desperately to rinse off in the store's employee shower, but things had already been set into motion. Within a few minutes, a couple police officers came inside the office. They observed him, sitting in a comfortable rolling chair, leaning back with his glasses off. Paul's vision was blurry, but he hoped his sight could be made perfect in the series of events about to happen

The cops looked like dark blue blurs, except for the man closest to him. He was tall, bald, black and compassionate. Perhaps he had dealt with people like Paul before, but this thought did not cross the young man's mind. Instead, he was still pre-occupied with the prospect of getting into that shower (*it would feel so good*), but the police were not having it. Instead, they calmly blocked his way and convinced him to sit back in the rolling chair.

Paul's spirits had not diminished. The cocktail of neuro-chemicals rushing through his brain were creating a kind of euphoria he had never experienced before. Eventually, the paramedics arrived. When questioned about his condition, the simplest explanation Paul could come up with was to tell them "I took some 'shrooms." Why Paul said this, he didn't know, but it seemed easier than explaining that he was either having some kind of mental breakdown, or was indeed some kind of shaman experiencing a prophetic vision (Paul suspected it was a combination of both possibilities).

By the time the ambulance doors slammed shut, Paul felt relief. Whether for good or ill, things had changed. The psychedelic climax of the episode was over, and the longest sleep in more than a week was about to follow. Paul could rest.

AURORA

My companions followed me
  Out of a wooden apartment door and
Black iron gate that swung shut behind us
  Announcing our departure with an abrupt metallic
  Farewell

The movie theater was a dozen blocks North
  I couldn't resist walking them past the discarded
Syringe cast aside on our sidewalk
  It excited me to find concrete evidence

Justifying the reputation our neighborhood has earned
  One of junkies, hookers--people
 Considered disposable, leaving proof of themselves
  In what they dispose of so easily

Dordji and Kelly led once we got past the
  Needle and followed the cars rushing past us on
Aurora--neon signs glimmered in the night like
  Sirens calling to the drivers, but my eyes dazzled too

How convenient for the junkies and the hookers
  To walk this broad boulevard, working
At once for life and death, making themselves
  Victims of their own crimes, neighbors unscathed

I can only afford to live in this neighborhood because
  Their dark habits resist the influx of moneyed denizens
I will enjoy neon signs, movie theaters, friends, comfort
  You don't destroy yourself on my behalf

  Thanks for letting me reap some reward
  Undisturbed

Part II

Horrible sanity

I became insane, with long intervals of horrible sanity.

-Edgar Allen Poe

They're coming for you, Barbara! They're coming for you!
Look, here comes one of them now!

-From *Night of the Living* by George Romero

THE GOOD
THE BAD
AND THE DEAD

Mitchell Rhodes sat counting aphids. One of his roles in the grow-house was to keep its eco-system in balance. If the number of insects, plants, or fungi was lopsided, he'd have to use pesticides, and he didn't like that. Beneath the cool light of an LED bulb, Rhodes finished his count. The row of plants had an average of 0.6 aphids each, well within the acceptable range. The egg plants and bell peppers nearby helped to repel them. He used his pen to scratch his scalp, leaned back in his chair, and looked around.

Each small grow house was made from a converted subway car. Each car focused on a different family of plants or a single crop. They stretched for more than a mile. The subway had become the community's new home. "The community" (always in lower-case) was the informal name of the Brooklyn Republic, a few tens of thousands survivors who'd hidden underground ever since the outbreak. In one and a half decades, they'd created a new home among the subway tunnels, sealed off from the outside, a harsh surface-world infested with the living dead.

A knock on the door ended Rhodes' reverie. The entrance opened and someone looked in. "Mr. Rhodes, may I have a word with you?"

"Come inside, and close the door behind you. You're letting moisture out."

"Of course, my apologies." The man wore a crisp gray suit with black pinstripes. He had the smell of a politician about him. His thin smile split his lined face, and gray had begun to creep into the hair around his temples. Otherwise, his mane was dark brown, his skin pale, body tall and lean. "Allow me to introduce myself, Mr. Rhodes. I am Christopher Warwick. Councilmember Warwick. I'm your representative for the Brooklyn Republic."

"I don't remember voting for you," Rhodes continued making marks on his clip-board.

Warwick looked down at him. Rhodes appeared to be in his mid-thirties, dark of skin and hair. Well-built, had the look of an athlete. When he wasn't engaged in surface explorations as a member of the Brooklyn Free Militia, he devoted most of his time to the grow-houses. Ninety-five percent of the Republic's food was grown or raised underground, due to the efforts of men and women like

Rhodes who made it possible.

"I see you're not for small talk. Okay, I'll get right to the point. I have a group of scientists synthesizing a new drug. They think it could be used for bites, to prevent infection, perhaps even reverse it."

"You mean bites from the infected?"

"Of course. The infected, the walking dead, zombies, whatever euphemism you want to use: those deceased bodies reanimated by viral parasite, HX-27, a.k.a. the zombie virus. Your feigned ignorance is tedious. The point is these scientists need a drug they don't have. I know you're planning a surface raid soon. You and your motley crew always are. Think you could find it for me?"

Rhodes let out a sound that was part laugh, part sigh. In his deep baritone, he rumbled, "What's in it for me?"

"A lot. A whole lot, for you, your crew, for our entire community. For you personally, I could think of any number of things: food, weapons, drugs, vitamins. Whatever you want. If this experimental medicine is a success, everyone involved will be rich beyond their wildest dreams. Even if it's not, I'll make the trouble worth your time."

Rhodes pondered for a moment. Warwick waited patiently, his gaze focused on Rhodes' dense, wooly mane, the sheen of his skin under the LED lamp. His mind considered other options in case Rhodes declined.

"I'll do it," Rhodes finally spoke. "But I have conditions. Yours will be a secondary objective. Our own mission comes first. Second, I pick my own crew. Third, our business is strictly confidential. And finally, if I find out you're fucking with me...well. I don't need to say what happens then."

"Likewise, Mr. Rhodes. Neither of us is to be trifled with."

The pair nodded, and shook hands. Warwick's grip was surprisingly hard; Rhodes' exuded a determined strength. They shared no pleasantries, but made arrangements for communicating details. One of Warwick's underlings would deliver a file containing details for the proposed operation. Rhodes was to share the information with no one except for the other members of his crew, then burn the file once the mission was complete.

After Warwick left, Rhodes tried to shift his concentration back to the business of the grow-house, but he couldn't focus. Instead, he went back to his chambers to wait for Warwick's correspondence. After an hour of reading and a meal of baked beans cooked on a hot-plate, the file finally arrived. It contained the precise whereabouts of a drug, Delphinium Hydroxide Pseudoephedrine, or D.H.P. The drug's name came from its active ingredient. According to the file, it had been developed as an experimental vaccine for H.I.V., a disease whose importance had diminished in the aftermath of the zombie outbreak.

The medicine had been in clinical trial at Brooklyn Medical University, known in the community as BMU. Retrieving it would be fairly easy; the only drugs that were difficult to find in pharmacies were opiates, but that challenge had been eased by the growth of poppy in the grow-houses. Rhodes examined the file in detail, but discovered no reason to be suspicious. His instincts told him not to trust Warwick, but that had more to do with his own prejudices than anything in the realm of fact.

Rhodes began to call together the squad he planned to bring with him. Tracking them down was sometimes tedious using land-lines, but there was no cell phone reception in the abandoned subway tunnels his community occupied. Luckily, they could still be used in the field.

Rhodes called Dr. Neal Hester first. Dr. Hester was his medical officer, a resident at the time of the initial outbreak. Now in his forties, the man was still in excellent physical condition due to a strict diet and exercise regimen. He was also an excellent marksman. Next, he spoke to Ms. Latisha Freeman. Latisha was his technical officer, adept at lock-picking, hacking, and equipment. She also controlled communications, keeping her team in contact with the community. Phil Eastman was in charge of demolitions and munitions. His father was an NYPD officer and survivalist; he taught Phil everything he knew and now lived in a remote cabin in the Catskills. Finally, Rhodes tracked down Sylvia Ramon, a woman whose assault and rape as a teenager had inspired her to become a master of hand to hand and small arms combat. She could be a little wild, but that was good sometimes.

"Ladies and gentlemen. Good to see you again," Rhodes welcomed them. His cigar smoke drifted through the light of a projector he'd connected to his laptop. It's display lit a white sheet hanging on the wall. His cloud of smoke pooled with the haze created by the joint Ramon, Hester and Eastman were passing back and forth; Freeman's cigarette added a hint of menthol. For this reason, he'd installed an exhaust fan in the room years ago.

"Good to see you, boss," Eastman said.

"Yeah, yeah. When do we get to waste some fuckin' Z's? Been gettin' restless," Ramon said, wiping her machete with an oil cloth and inspecting its edge.

"I'll get to that. If you'll let me." A shrug from her shoulders told him it was okay to move on. Rhodes tapped a button of his laptop, and a satellite image appeared. "This is the intersection of West Lafayette and 64th." Another click. "An abandoned drug store and pharmacy." Click. "And this is a bottle of neo-natal vitamins, the primary objective for our mission. Ramon, remind your less educated colleagues what neo-natal vitamins are for."

"Babies," she explained. "They're for women having babies."

"I knew that," Eastman scoffed.

"Shut up, Phil. Go on, Mr. Rhodes," Hester prompted.

"Thanks, Doc. As we know, the U.V. lights and tomatoes in our diet have eliminated the need for gathering so much of vitamins C and D. But these neo-natals are crucial for lowering infant mortality. Of course, if you see anything else useful, you're welcome to grab it, but we don't want to make our packs too heavy, because we'll be making one more stop." Rhodes' finger tapped one more time. "Brooklyn Medical University, better known as BMU. There's an office in the Cooper Building we need to visit."

"Rhodes, we cleared Cooper a few months ago. Remember that stash of morphine?" Freeman reminded him.

"Thanks, Latisha, but we're looking for something else this time. An experimental drug called D.H.P. I have a source representing a group of concerned scientists who want to synthesize this drug into something we can use. It was made to fight H.I.V., but my source says the eggheads in R&D can turn it into a drug that could prevent the zombie virus, perhaps even cure it."

Ramon let out a low whistle. "I'm sure you realize," Rhodes continued, "this could be our most important mission ever. Not to mention the payment we'll receive for recovering it. The reason it's not our primary objective is because this whole operation is hush-hush. No loose lips. That means 'shut the fuck up'. Got it?" They nodded, except Ramon who rolled her eyes.

"Hell, this might be the job that lets us retire, but first we need to bring the drug back, and come back ourselves. I don't need to remind you what happened to John Jakes."

"Christ," Ramon muttered. "Johnny."

"The mission starts at 0900, tomorrow, Friday the thirteenth of October, in case you haven't been keeping a calendar. We rendezvous at the steps leading up to Piedmont station. Come armed, come ready. Any questions?"

* * * * *

The light shining into Piedmont blinded them for a moment. Eastman led the squad up a long stairway, and Rhodes brought up the rear. They heard the *clack* from the metal doors being shut behind them, then the grinding of a lock. Even after they put on their shades, it still took a minute for their eyes to adjust to the intensity of sunshine. It was good they waited, because Freeman spotted a runner as soon as they reached the top of the steps. "Eastman, watch your three," she spoke.

"On it," he replied. The man drew a .45 Magnum, aimed, and blew the zombie's head clean off. "Any others?" The rank smell of decay filled the air.

Dr. Hester scanned the perimeter with his scoped rifle while the others looked around. "Just some walkers, but they're not too keen on us yet." A few corpses upwind shuffled aimlessly.

"Good," Rhodes said. His companions lowered their guns and began walking from the stairway. The Brooklyn autumn was bursting in color, and uncollected leaves shuffled with each footstep.

A loud, gibbering of word-like noises erupted behind them, and the squad turned just in time to see another runner leap from the the top of a bus stop that had been hidden from view. No one was able to raise their guns in time, but Ramon brought up her machete and split its skull. "Bindejo..." she cursed, and wiped its black blood on a few fallen leaves.

"That's why we always need to check our perimeter thoroughly," Rhodes told them.

"Yeah? I didn't see your eyes on our six either," Eastman growled through clenched teeth.

"Cool it. He means from now on," Freeman told him.

"Freeman," Rhodes asked, "where we headed?"

Latisha checked the GPS app she'd installed on her cell phone, one of the "smart" models popular a couple of decades ago. It worked, so that meant somewhere people were still in control of the commercial satellites, at least a few of them. Her own community activated and maintained a half-dozen cell phone towers in Brooklyn. According to the GPS app, their destination was four miles northeast, on the edge of Williamsburg. "This way," she announced, and led the squad east along the shadows of the row houses.

Every few blocks, Dr. Hester used his sniper rifle to take out runners who would come sprinting from hundreds of feet away. A few curious walkers were handled by Ramon's machete, Eastman's hammer, or Freeman's katana. Rhodes wielded a trench knife, but engaged in hand to hand combat only in emergencies. Once, walkers came in four directions, threatening to swarm, but Eastman found some high ground and dropped a couple grenades that took out the entire group. The explosion vibrated in their chests, and the ashes tasted bitter.

Eventually, they found the sign for the drug store above a couple sliding doors that led inside a concrete building. The entry glass had shattered. "Flashlights," Rhodes reminded them. They each turned on lights attached to the barrels of their guns, and tactical head-lamps that shined in the direction of their view.

Rhodes pumped his shot-gun with and announced, "I'll take point. Eastman, bring up the rear. If you need to use a frag, tell us. I don't want to pick shrapnel out of my ass tonight."

"Got it, boss."

Rhodes entered the drug store's dim interior. Glass crunched with each measured step. A few shuffles and groans could be heard coming from the darkness. "Good. They've been hibernating. I want a pincer sweep down the sides. We'll corral them in the center, wipe them out. Remember to watch your six, and don't forget to keep an eye out for each other."

Rhodes and Ramon walked down the left side of the store; Eastman, Hester, and Freeman took the right. They moved down every aisle, prodding each sluggish walker toward the middle of the store, and eliminating the more eager ones with blade or hammer. Each member of the militia packed long, collapsible metal batons that could be used to push walkers from a distance. Those waking from hibernation usually didn't put up much resistance. Sleep was better than starvation, but their repose became a disadvantage when they were in the militia's way.

"Mmm, baby food," Freeman murmured. She tossed a couple glass jars into a messenger bag strapped around her shoulder. "Dessert."

"They grow pears now," Hester told her. "Fresh ones. They transplanted a couple trees from the surface to a tunnel on the west-side. You don't need to eat puree."

"Yeah," Freeman scoffed. "Only a carton of cigs or twenty bucks a pear. Baby food's cheaper."

Ramon's machete sunk into another skull. "Don't bother me. I know how to haggle." Black blood dripped from her blade.

In a few minutes, they'd huddled the zombies into a mass of bodies in a broad aisle that separated both sides of the store. "Phil, we're ready," Rhodes told him.

"Frag out!" Eastman warned. The heavy metallic clunk of the grenades preceded the explosions by a few seconds.

"All right, mop 'em up," Rhodes ordered. A few gunshots and blade-strokes were all it took to destroy the rest. "Damn, that's a hot mess. Good work, everybody."

A gun-shot rang out from the front of the store. "Fuck!" Eastman roared, and fell to the ground. He held his left arm against his body, and fired a pistol with his right, aiming wildly in the direction of the bullet that had struck him. The clap of the shots became a primal war-beat.

"Everyone hit the floor!" Ramon yelled.

"Doc, check him out," Rhodes said.

"On it."

A few scavengers had been attracted by the noise from their weapons. They wore badly worn clothes, and some carried pistols. One held a rifle. Others carried knives, chains, metal pipes and other improvised weapons. "Cons," Rhodes hissed, "by the look of them."

"Come to get their revenge," Freeman warned.

"I'll make 'em wish they'd stayed gone," Ramon brought around her AR-15 and rolled out of cover, firing as she walked across the center aisle, blasting everything in front of her, including any cons caught in the path of her bullet storm. But then three shots hit her torso, and she went to the ground.

"Damn! They got Sylvia," Freeman cursed.

"How many left?" Rhodes asked.

Freeman brought up an extendable mirror from her pack. "Four," she whispered. "Coming this way."

Rhodes raised his fingers, counting silently. *One. Two.* On three, he nodded.

They turned into the aisle, and let loose. Both barrels of Rhodes' shot-gun blasted into the crowd of scavengers, but one who avoided his buck shot's brunt was brought down by a pair of Berettas. Freeman wielded in each hand. "God damn..." Rhodes sighed.

"Uh, boss? No wounds," Doc Hester helped Ramon back onto her feet.

"What the fuck." Rhodes gaped.

Ramon giggled. "Kevlar," she explained. "Got it from a police station a few weeks ago."

Rhodes slapped her hard across the face. "You got a death wish, take care of it on your own time. Otherwise, you stay in cover 'til I order you out. You don't get to die without my permission."

Silvia's eyes burned. She touched the side of her cheek, but said nothing.

Rhodes asked the doc, "How's Eastman?"

"Not bad," Hester assured him. "The bullet went right through his left bicep, but it didn't strike bone. The wound'll be weeping. For a while, at least. I disinfected it, wrapped him with a bandage, gave him a coagulant, but it'll be a while before the bleeding stops completely."

"Damn, why couldn't you get it through the skull so we could've just *left* you here?" Ramon cursed. "They can smell blood for miles."

"You need to shut up," Freeman told her.

"You gonna make me?" Ramon challenged.

"I just might. You front like a scared little boy. Got anything to back it up with?"

Ramon stared up at her. Freeman didn't flinch. Rhodes moved between them and pushed them apart. "Enough bullshit!" he swore. "We got a mission to worry about. Ramon, I don't need to hear nothing out of your mouth except 'Yes sir, no sir,' for the rest of the mission. Anything else, I take your rations for a week."

Ramon stayed silent. "Ain't so tough now," Freeman muttered.

"Same goes for you!" Rhodes barked. "Now c'mere, and help me look for those damn vitamins." He brought Freeman with him behind the pharmacy's counter.

Ramon sat on the floor next to Eastman and Doc Hester. She lit an LED lantern she carried in her back-pack and set it on the floor in front of them. The others turned off their gun and head lamps to save battery. Ramon brought out a joint she'd tucked behind her ear, lit it, and inhaled. Smoke left through her nose, and she held it out to Eastman.

"Thanks," he said, and took a hit. "Doc?"

"You're god damned right," Doc said, and took a long drag.

"You know," Eastman spoke, "Rhodes is under a lot of pressure when we're out here. You ought to lay off him. Latisha too."

"How the hell else am I supposed to have any fun with 'em?" Ramon asked. "You knew it was a fuckin' joke."

"Any more jokes, you're gonna end up down a zombie's throat," Doc Hester told her. "Good shit, by the way."

"Thanks," she said. "Got a couple plants growing. Rhodes ain't the only one gotta green thumb."

Rhodes and Freeman returned. "Got what we came for," he told his crew. "Now let me hit that." Rhodes held it between his thumb and index finger, and inhaled. "Freeman?" he asked as he held the smoke in.

"Thanks," she took it, drew in 'til she nearly singed her fingers, then flicked the roach onto the pile of bodies nearby.

"Hope everyone feels a little better now. Gonna be a bit of a hike to BMU, but Freeman found a route through the subway. Not in the settled tunnels, but there'll be less zombies than here on the surface."

Ramon, Eastman, and Hester rose, and they walked back outside into the bright chill of autumn. Around the corner, Latisha led them to another subway station, and they began their descent back into the darkness.

The unsettled subway tunnels were restless. Hibernating zombies woke and clawed against the glass of the locked cars. A few windows shattered, but so many undead tried to pull through at the same time, the group passed them by before any got a chance to pursue them.

They trekked five miles through the tunnels until they climbed back up to the surface. The afternoon sun burned their eyes, so they put their glasses back on and explored the medical campus. Walkers in scrubs shambled around the grounds, but by then Eastman's wound had stopped bleeding and Hester had changed his dressings, so they weren't swarmed. Instead, they simply eluded the zombies, and any that too curious or unavoidable were taken care of.

Cooper Building was unlocked. A good sign, because if any scavengers had cooped themselves inside, their mission would only get bloodier. Rhodes brought his group up the steps of the building, and Freeman led them toward the experimental lab.

"In here," she pointed. The lab's door was emblazoned with an orange bio-hazard symbol. Latisha examined the entryway. "An electronic lock. And there's no power."

"Can you hack it?" Rhodes asked.

"Yeah, give me a minute," she told him. Latisha brought a crowbar from her pack, and pried off the metal panel protecting the lock's mechanism. Next, she used an ignite socket, a makeshift device that would power the lock and let her to open it. "Now it just depends on how much time it takes to crack the security code. Shouldn't be long."

In a few moments, the door unlocked, but an alarm began to howl. Red lights flashed in the hallway. "God damn it! Shut it off before we're swarmed!" Rhodes bellowed.

"I'm trying, but I've been shut out. They must have an emergency generator on stand-by to power the security system," Freeman said. "I'm must've triggered it when I powered on the lock."

"Christ," Ramon uttered. "We're fucked."

"Not yet," Eastman said. "Doc, help me barricade the staircase."

"On it." Hester broke off the leg of a chair and placed it between the doors' handles, bracing them shut. Then the pair pulled a couple of book-cases, full of texts, over to block the doorway. They tipped them, and laid them side by side on top of each other. "Should buy us *some* time at least."

"Good," Rhodes said. "Alright, only one way from here."

Rhodes opened the door to the experimental lab, and a zombie in a biohazard suit came rushing out. It caught a double-blast of buckshot from his shotgun, and then Rhodes pulled the door shut again, but not before he saw that the room was crowded with undead. The alarm continued to blare, and Rhodes peered out the window. Already a swarm of walkers surrounded the entire structure. Behind them, a thunderous beating began against the door leading up from the stairwell.

"Looks like we're in the middle of a shit sandwich," Ramon remarked.

"Get ready to take a bite," Eastman told her.

"Phil, how many grenades you got left?" Rhodes asked.

"Three."

"Take two, and pull the pins when I signal. I'm gonna open the door, you'll toss them in, just a few feet. We let them blow, then go in, guns blazing. Don't stop killing until they're all destroyed."

"Or we are," Ramon offered as an alternative.

"Take point, Ramon," Rhodes instructed.

"Glad to," She held her machete in one hand; her other gripped the AR-15 strapped to her shoulder.

"Everybody got their head lamps on?" Rhodes asked. "Alright, let's do this. Three, two..." Rhodes pushed the door open, Eastman dropped his frags, and pulled the door shut. A muffled *boom boom* echoed, then Ramon ran into the room, swinging her machete and spraying lead. The rest of them came in behind her.

The waves of dead seemed endless. Old professors in lab-coats, students in scrubs, scientists in sealed bio-hazard suits torn open by hunger; all surged forward, and all fell. The group formed a tight circle near the entrance of the room and continued firing.

"Ramon, Freeman, Hester, re-load. Latisha, pour it on," Rhodes ordered. The clack of dropped magazines could be heard, then the click of re-loaded weapons. "Okay, our turn," he said, and put another couple shells in his shotgun, the rungs of the trench knife still around one fist in case any zombies came too close.

"Think they're thinning out, boss," Eastman yelled over the gun blaze.

"Keep shooting!" Ramon hissed.

Behind them, the door into the lab opened, and five runners charged in. The group retreated behind an overturned desk, but not before one of them took a chunk out of Eastman's thigh. He screamed, and fired his Magnum until the one who bit him was only a puddle of fluid and flesh, but the ragged bite that had torn through clothes and skin made his eyes go wide for a moment.

"I'm a dead man," Eastman whispered.

"Not yet," Rhodes countered. "If we recover the D.H.P. and bring it back to R&D, they might be able to give you a cure before you turn."

"Not likely," Eastman chuckled grimly. He pulled himself above the desk and fired back into the remaining crowd of walkers still pushing themselves inside. For a moment, they struggled against the crowd that had formed, frustrating their endless hunger.

"Lock the door behind me?" Eastman asked, and climbed over the bodies back out into the hallway, firing the his last bullets. Freeman and Rhodes held the door shut against the swarm while Freeman punched buttons on the security key-pad. The lock clicked shut. A muffled explosion rumbled through the door. Then silence fell like a veil.

"Jesus Christo," Ramon murmured, making a sign of the cross.

"Let's mourn when we get back," Rhodes told them. "We still got a job to do. Freeman, come with me."

Freeman followed him back into the lab's synthesizing room, and the pair found what they were looking for. It was fairly plain; just a white bottle with a typed label. Inside, it was filled with white caplets. "A lot of trouble for a bottle of medicine," she said.

"If it does what it's supposed to, it'll mean a lot more than that."

Freeman nodded, and walked out the lab's entrance. She swore she saw Ramon wipe tears from her face, but couldn't be certain. "We got it," she told them.

"Alright, everybody. Hard part's over," Rhodes said. "According to intel, there's another stairwell from inside this lab that leads up to the roof. We're going to call in aerial extraction. Paramedic helicopters running out of Brooklyn General. One of 'em will bring us back to Piedmont."

His words were met with a cold silence. Ramon led them through the door to the stairwell, hacking through the skull of a zombie that was only a crawling torso. Hester shuddered and cursed.

"Ramon, you think you could give me some of those greens you got growing when we get back?" he asked.

"I got you, Doc."

The door leading out from the stairwell hadn't been locked. When they got out onto the rooftop they could see why. A rope made out of lab-coats still hung, clinging to a ventilation pipe. It led back down to the street below.

"Freeman, radio for extraction," Rhodes ordered.

"Already on it," she responded. Freeman erected a small portable antenna, and began speaking into a C.B. radio. Ramon turned a small generator crank that kept it powered. Doc Hester lit a smoke flare, and held it out to his side. Rhodes walked over to the ledge of the building and looked out. Zombies still swarmed, trampling each other, enraged by the scent of living flesh. He spit off the ledge, and turned back to the group, shaking his head.

"ETA, five minutes, boss," Freeman announced.

Rhodes nodded, and pulled a flask from the inside of his pack. "Was gonna save this until we got back, but I guess it's as good a time as any." He unscrewed the lid, and poured some kind of liquor onto the roof. "For Phil. And John Jakes." Then he took a swig, and winced. "Mmm, *mmm*." He passed the bottle to Doc Hester. "Ain't no bathroom swill neither. That's some fine Kentucky bourbon."

"Thanks, Rhodes," Doc Hester took a long pull, and passed it to Freeman as he wiped his chin. Freeman drank, winced, and passed the flask to Ramon, who passed it back to Rhodes after drinking some herself.

Rhodes took another sip, screwed its cap back on, and returned it to his pack. In the distance, they could hear the hum of a helicopter's blades. Hester began to wave the smoke flare back and forth. The helicopter turned, and approached. As it hovered overhead, a rope-ladder dropped, and Ramon gripped it, pulling herself up followed by the others.

Once they were airborne, Rhodes brought the flask back out. He passed it around, and asked the machine gunner if he'd like to finish it off. The pilot nodded his approval, and the gunner grinned, and drained the flask. "Thanks, hoss."

Rhodes looked out at Brooklyn, laid out beneath them for miles. The evening sun cloaked half the city in shadow, while the other half burned bright. The autumn leaves made it seem like the whole city was on fire, and Rhodes imagined it was so.

"The walkers can have the whole god-damned thing."

* * * * *

Warwick met Rhodes after the de-briefing. He smiled and laid a black briefcase out onto a table. He unclasped it with a *click, click* then opened it wide. Mason jars full of psilocybin mushrooms, blotter acid, vitamins, sardine cans, five marijuana blunts, a large bag of cocaine, and a few bottles of antibiotics were nestled inside.

"Payday," Rhodes said, rubbing his palms together.

"Just the tip of the iceberg, Mr. Rhodes," Warwick promised. "That drug you recovered is going to make us rich beyond our wildest dreams."

"They already synthesized a cure?" Rhodes asked.

"Only a cure for melancholy," Warwick told him. "Delphinum Hydroxide Pseudophedrine is a necessary ingredient for synthesizing methamphetamines. D.H.P. is the most pure source of pseudophedrine we could find, ever since the scavengers and meth-heads ripped off all the drug stores for cold medicine. We burned through our supplies weeks ago, but now our scientists can break it down, and we'll synthesize our own."

"You sent us on a meth run? You were fucking with us the whole *time*?" Rhodes seethed.

"I told you I'd make it worth your while. The lie was simply meant to salve your conscience. You're the best soldier the Republic has, but you have some very inconvenient scruples."

"I lost a good man out there. Don't you remember what I said would happened if you *fucked* me?!" Rhodes gripped Warwick's throat with one meaty hand. Warwick choked, and pressed a pistol against Rhodes' stomach. He released him.

"I'll forgive you for that, Mr. Rhodes," Warwick spoke in a ragged breath. "I'd heard you lost a soldier even before you told me. You have my sympathies. Certainly the contents of this briefcase is a small consolation. And only a small taste of what's yet to come."

Rhodes stared at Warwick with a look of pure hatred. "I'm only asking for your silence." Warwick continued. He brought the pistol back down to his side. Rhodes walked up to him, and stared into the pale man's cold blue eyes. In a single movement, he brought up his trench knife and tore through Warwick's bowels. Warwick fired his pistol three times.

* * * * *

Ramon heard the shots from inside her room. She tucked a Beretta into the waistband of her sweatpants and opened the door of her subway car. She looked up and down the tracks, but no one else was around. Rhodes' car was next to her own, so she knocked on his door. No answer. She tested the lock, and it was open, so she slid it wide and pulled herself inside, her gun held out in front of her.

"Rhodes, you okay?" She entered and found Rhodes and Warwick bleeding on the floor.

"Ain't that a damn shame," she muttered, looking into Rhodes glassy eyes. She closed them with her fingers and made a sign of the cross, kissing her pistol when she finished.

She looked inside the briefcase, understood its contents, closed its clasps, and picked it up. Warwick whimpered on the floor, begging her for mercy. Ramon ignored him. She took one quick glance around the room and found Rhodes' trench knife resting on a table. She picked it up, took it with her.

"I best be ramblin' on."

AMERICAN FANTASTIC & THE CREATIVE COMMUNITY
PROUDLY PRESENT THE

NIGHT OF THE CHUPACABRA

AN EVENING OF WORDS WRITTEN AND SPOKEN,
MUSIC, ART, AND MARVELS OF ALL KINDS

OPEN MIC AND FEAUTURED WRITER, JOHN BEECHEM 6-7 PM
MUSICAL MERRIMENT WITH MAPLEX MONK & DR. ROCKWELL 7-8 PM
DJ MYTHOS OF ARTXFM'S THE MYTHIC BEAT 8-9 PM

TACO PUNK
FRIDAY AUGUST 15TH, 6-9 P.M.
736 E MARKET ST., LOUISVILLE, KY

AMERICANFANTASTIC.COM MAPLEXMONK.COM MIXCLOUD.COM/MYTHICBEAT/

NIGHT OF THE CHUPACABRA

At a bar in Juarez
Where the tequila is
As salty as the tears
A man sits alone, but
For his drink

His bourbon speaks to him
In the clink of ice cubes
Its glass a cool breath
On his hand this
Hot August night
A sweaty palm
Touches his back
Without looking
He pushes himself from
The splintery bar

'Chupacabra,' a voice speaks
'Another full moon.
Come, it is time.'

Luna's naked eye follows them down
Streets and alleys until they come
To the truck-yard, chain-linked
Full of emptiness, vacant freight
Except for one grand 16-wheeler

Chupacabra examines the burden
Carried inside her steel womb
Fifty kilos of cocaina, powdered ferocity
Ten kilos of marijuana, sticky daydreams

Twenty kilos of heroina, blissful oblivion
Fifteen kids, teenagers most of them

'And who are they?' Chupacabra asks.

'They are $10,000 American dollars. Do as
you are told, hombre. No questions.'

Chupacabra nods, slides down the door of the trailer
Beats his knuckles against it.

'Vaya con dios,' he hears dimly
As he takes the wheel
Pulls out into the night
Following the stars like
An ancient magi
North to Texas
Land of guns and gringos

From time to time,
A car or truck drives behind them
Down this lonely road
They are toll collectors
One from the Juarez cartel
In a gleaming white pick-up truck
The policia come in a black SUV
Neither looks the chupacabra in the eye
They keep one eye on the money
Another on the moon

He understands their fear
He has lost his taste for cows and sheep
Since so many men are so much more
Worthy of his claws and fangs

Yet he still is a man, usually
So he must make a living
He drives for hours

On the endless highway
To the corridor
His employers have paid to use
On the way
He stops
In the shadow of a mesa

He pulls down then up on the
Chain hooked to the trailer's door
The young ones stare at him
Their eyes half-blinded by the moonlight
'Que pasa?' Chupacabra asks
Baño. Now. Water. Quick.
We are hidden.
But must cross before the sunrise.'

They nod and
Follow his instructions
Chupacabra watches as they leave
Checking faces for bruises
He did not notice before he left Juarez
It is fortunate for his passengers
He does not find any

The boys and girls
Divide into two groups
And rain two tiny oases

Chupacabra finds his own space
Does the same
Then stands by his cab
Taps his foot
Like a jack-rabbit
Waiting with a
Fiery impatience
Five minutes have passed

At three-thirty they cross into Texas
A few score miles outside El Paso
Driving past a fallen cattle-fence
Across an otherwise invisible border

The radio begins to blur
Stations overlapping
Chupacabra turns it off
So he can concentrate
It does not help.
In a quarter of an hour,
Blue and red lights turn on
Surround him from black pick-up trucks
Minute men. Militia. One fires

A warning shot
Chupacabra slows to a stop
Rolls down the window
The desert's chill
Enters his cab
He puts on a flannel
Pulls down his hat's crooked bill
Over his black eyes

'You lost, amigo?' the cowboy asks
In hick English. Chupacabra understands
Pretends he does not. 'No hablo Ingles.'

'Ain't that a shame. Johnny! Open her up.'
The snap of a lock. The soft tinkle of a chain
Rattling wheels as the trailer door slides open.

'Well, I'll be god-damned!
Don't call it in, Rick.
 We're gonna have some
Fun first'

Chupacabra steps out of his cab
Drop to the ground with a soft thud
Held at the point of a shotgun
A clumsy weapon, the kind he has no need for
At least when the moon is full
They are leading the kids out of the trailer
One by one, they divide the boys and the girls
'Do not touch them,' Chupacabra calls
'I pay if they are hurt. *Es no bueno.*'

'Well, lookie who *habla Ingles* after all.
Don't worry, amigo, we won't hurt 'em. Too much.
Chupacabra takes a step toward his
Human cargo. He gets the butt of a rifle
In his belly for the effort and sinks to his knees.
One of the girls is crying. He hears the rip of
Fabric. The boys protest, but fall silent at the
Sound of gunshots fired into the air.

Chupacabra stares at the moon
And feels the change begin
His incisors grow too large for his mouth
So he opens it, and a long pointed tongue falls out
He feels his eyes turn yellow, and in the
Black of night, bursts of color appear in his vision
Where there are warm bodies.
Red, yellow and green, but the cold guns are still
Dark as midnight. He falls forward again
Puts his hands out to catch himself
Fingernails turning into claws, the hair on his
Arms and hands turning to fur, gray with black spots

Clothes fall to shreds as his muscles well and ripple
He feels his hackles rise and he can contain it
No longer. A howl erupts from his throat

It bears the sound of the coyote, the wolf, the
Wild dog, until it falls into the chaos
Of a hyena's laugh.
'What in Sam Hell?' One of the Minute-Men asks
Chupacabra lunges, and before the man can finish his thought
His life has ended like the life of most prey
Quick, messy, and beyond comprehension

Then the shots begin
The stinging scatter of a shotgun
A heavy boom from a rifle
The mad clapping of countless pistols
The desert's magic protects Chupacabra
He absorbs the metal stones that would kill
Him as a human, but sheds them instead to fall
Into the sand

The next moment is pure chaos
He tears one man's arm from his shoulder
His gun still firing RATATATAT
Into the darkness. A few flee into their trucks
But not all of them. One who had rape on his
Mind stumbles and falls, pants around his knees
Chupacabra takes his manhood in one gulp
And the only mercy left to him is a
Quick crunchy death

The children stare wide-eyed
Until one of the older girls leads them back into the trailer
Some are crying. Some have seen worse.
Prayers of thanks, prayers for protection, but
None for the dead
Eventually, the sounds stop. A weary man
Appears at the trailer's open door
His clothes in tatters, sweaty but so alive
He tosses a backpack and a half-dozen

Water bottles inside. From behind him
They can see the soft pink of an American sunrise
Without a word, he closes the hatch

Back in his cab, Chupacabra can still taste the blood
It's been five hundred years almost, but he can
Still remember the cold metal of the conquistador
The smoky muskets of Texans
And in his dim memories
The arrows and spears of the Aztec
Once the farmers gave him
Offerings to keep him from their herds
But now he is a shepherd, a coyote
El chupacabra

American Fantastic
proudly presents

The Cottonwood Curse
and other spooky tales

AmericanFantastic.com

Saturday October 17th
7-9 PM at Sunergos in Iroquois 306 W Woodlawn Ave
Open Mic Coffee Delightful Delicacies
Come give the Devil his Due

THE COTTONWOOD CURSE

I write these words as a man determined to die. My life is one of pain, despair, addiction, and darkness. To extinguish the spark of my life would be to smother a doomed flame, a flickering wick of grief trapped inside a human being. Its cessation would be a mercy. Not only to me, but to those whose lives are intertwined with the thread of my own.

The doctors tell me I am a mortal case, and I believe them. Three years ago, a sojourn to a drier clime would bring me a relief, if sometimes a stinging sunburn. Now it brings me nothing but frightened stares and bloody handkerchiefs. Consumption. The bloody lunged blighter grants her scarlet kiss to the just and the unjust alike, but I am more deserving of her greedy lips than any other, I'd wager.

In the grandstand, they situate themselves far from me now. I tire of staining countless linen scraps; now I simply tie a piece of silk around my face, laced with a touch of *parfum* to ward off the smell of manure. My family helped fund the construction of Churchill Downs, so even with my affliction, none dare turn me away.

Howard accompanies me. He oft reminisces about his boyhood labors in my father's stable, tells me which colt to place a bet on when my mind is too scattered to decide, and is quick to fetch bourbon and tobacco when the need arises. I allow him to take off his servant's coat on days that it is warm, and we roll up the sleeves of our shirts, and watch the races together. Although he is a son of Ham, Howard has a keen mind, and a serpent's tongue. He tells me God has damned me for the deeds I've done, and my crimes are so wicked, my life has become a hell on earth. "Just a warm breath compared to what waits for you, Mr. Bingham," he often taunts. I am inclined to agree. Howard Freeman is a bastard in every sense of the word, but I've grown fond of him. He's clever as far as bastards go, and in exchange for his care unto my death, I have written him the sum of

$7,000 to be bequeathed from my will, one that will provide well for his wife and their brood, which now numbers nine if my memory serves. Indeed, it is my cursed memory that torments me.

The evil night that plagues my mind was almost half a decade ago. It was in the final days of the Southern Exposition, illuminated by crackling electric lanterns swarmed by moths, a Saturday evening among the dozens of new mansions built in the past few years. Mine stands tall in Belgravia Court, built close to 4th Street for the convenience of our late cantankerous carriage driver, Howard's father Philip. God rest his soul, he is among the departed.

I digress. Please pardon the chaos of these scribbles; their meanderings are evidence of a scattered mind. Lilian was with me that night, my golden haired wife, at the height of beauty in her twenty-first year as I was entering my twenty-sixth. She was of Sanders stock, so her father and half her uncles were Kentucky Colonels. My father suggested our courtship, hungry for a large dowry, I've no doubt. He held me in contempt, the miserable old man, and knew the depths of my vices made me ill-suited for industrious work. My best hope, he always told me, was to charm a poor, little rich girl, one lonely and with a heart aching from loss. I followed his advice, and caught the eye of the young widow, Lilian Sanders, at a Wednesday night picnic the summer before my consumption became evident.

In half a dozen months we were wed, and in a display of wealth worthy of Midas, Lilian's father paid for the construction of our home as part of her dowry. I also received a quarter of the home's value in cash, in part to pay for our furnishings. The remainder was put into an account, a little nest egg for the both of us, to use when we started producing heirs of our own. This would provide for education at the university, finery to distinguish their level of birth, and other trappings of wealth in this so-called Gilded Age.

This excess was evident that night at the Exposition. We were newlyweds out for a night-time stroll. Our ears were piqued by the sound of a melodious guitar, one plucked by skilled and nimble hands. A young black man in a bright blue suit, his eyes twinkling with the mischief of a dandy, was playing "Oberon". It was a song he played often and well. His father had been one of Justin Holland's apprentices. My wife stopped, and we turned to listen. His gaze caught Lilian's eye and he bowed his head. The tune abruptly switched, and he strummed a song with lyrics sprung from cupid's heart. He had a mythical talent, that is to be sure, but all the pluck of the gods as well, to make such a bold display before my own wife.

In a flash of hot anger, I pulled Lilian away from him, and we walked down Park Avenue to meet my bookie, Charles Dorsey. He owed me money for a wager I'd made on a ball game between Louisville and Cincinnati; the local boys lost (as I knew they would–I had made specific arrangements) and I was about to collect a tidy sum. Lilian was annoyed by my gambling habit, but it made her secret love of the poppy less damning, so in a tenuous truce, we had agreed to discuss neither. However, she began to protest as we left the guitar player far behind.

"Damn you, Robert! That boy was splendid. Why don't you ever want to stop and listen to the world for a moment?" Her anger was palpable, if a bit silly.

I sighed, and pulled a pocket watch from my black vest. I flipped its gold lid, checked the time, and explained, "Dorsey said 9:00 P.M. It's a quarter to the hour, and I find it prudent to collect on my wager before his other debtors come calling. Forget the darkie; I'll get Howard to play his banjo for us tonight."

"I'm tired of Howard's songs," she sighed, and looked behind us at the colored Casanova.

I tugged harder, and he was soon lost from view.

* * * * *

At the stroke of three, I awoke and felt my bed empty. Lilian and I slept together every night. After I satisfied my masculine desires, with an empathic rapidity, I would roll onto my back and sleep. If I woke to fill the chamber pot, Lilian would be asleep, curled away from me. Tonight, she was absent.

I pulled my robe on, and grabbed a pistol from my bureau. Where had she gone?

I found them in the billiard room. The cries of their beastly coitus could be heard from the library. The room had a lock, but as master of the house, I carry a skeleton key with me at all times. In case a member of weaker sex is to find and recover this journal, I will spare your fragile heart the details, but let it be said, their debauchery would have made Bacchus and Venus proud.

The pair stopped, their eyes turned toward me. The young musician turned from my wife and faced me, pulling his blue breeches back on and tying his belt. His arousal made this a difficult task, to say the least.

My wife made no attempt at modesty, and laughed cruelly. "Guitar ain't the only thing he's good at. Is that pistol even loaded?"

I remember nothing but my vision flooding red. In a moment, my ears were deafened by the crack of the pistol, and when I opened my eyes, Lilian's blood and brains were spread upon the pool table. I looked at the smoking gun in my hand, and felt a moment of dread. Then the dark machinations of my mind began to turn, and I thought of a scheme.

I struck the guitar player's face with the butt of my pistol. Abraham Greene; I would learn his name when I read the newspaper the next morning. The boy fell to the floor, and I picked him up by his ruffled collar. "You're coming with me, Orpheus."

With the barrel of the pistol at his back, I directed Abraham to the door. I kicked him down the steps, and looked at the bemused crowd of revelers gathering on the walkway in front of my home. They were strolling by, revelers who had left the Exposition and were on their way home. "This man slew my wife!" I roared. "He came into my home, raped my darling Lilian, and with his lustful thirst slaked, put a bullet into her head. What say ye, gentlemen, ye sons of the Confederacy?" A few turned away, shaking their heads, and cursing. Half a dozen young men looked up at Abraham, their liquored eyes glazed with bloodlust.

A member of the local constabulary, soaked to the gills but with a yeoman's constitution, came up to us both. "This one's not fit for the courtroom. We'll have our vengeance now."

We formed a mob, and marched north to the Floral Terrace. To the lynching tree. Someone had grabbed a rope, and then the dandy's face was wrought in a coward's acceptance of death. He cried and wailed, calling for his mother, staring at me with pleading eyes. In minutes, we reached the tree, a tall cottonwood. I grinned, poking him in the chest with the pistol's barrel as the rope was tightened around his neck. The constable threw it over one of the limbs, and a trio of brawny men pulled Abraham high into the air.

His death did not take long. When it was over, when I was certain, I fired a pair of shots into the air, and returned home. I told Howard to allow the magistrates to enter the estate, and arrange to have Lilian's body taken away. I made arrangements to contact her father.

* * * * *

The following five years were spent in bleak misery. After Lilian's death, I spent much of her father's fortune in the brothels. I was intelligent enough to protect myself against Nature's punishment for fornication, but tuberculosis came to me instead. In the remaining years of my life, I vowed, I would have a lifetime's worth of experiences. I traveled down the Mississippi in an opulent steamship, sailed near Cuba and the Bahamas, drank absinthe by the crate, smoked hashish by the pound, and gambled my life's fortune away. It did nothing but numb the pain, which would inevitably return.

And so I waited for my life to end.

Three days ago, I began to hear the tune of Oberon played from outside. I would shut my bedroom's window, but the song would not cease. Even with the bellowing of a trumpet in my parlor or my ears plugged with wax, nothing could push the dreaded melody from my mind.

But this night, I have found it. I have traced its source, in the light of the full moon, to that tree in Floral Terrace. I walked the blocks north in my bed-robe, my pistol to protect me from scoundrels, and my journal to record my observations. As soon as I viewed the blonde leaved-tree, the sounds of Oberon ceased as suddenly as if a conductor had willed it.

I stared up into the branches of the tall cottonwood. Somewhere an owl hooted, and a bat flew from its arboreal perch, into a cloud of bugs basking in Luna's glow. I saw Abraham, hanging. I see him now. No longer corporeal, his spirit glows a dim blue. Abraham's clothes are tattered, but his face is no longer tear-streaked. He looks down at me, impatiently.

In front of the trunk, someone has placed a pile of black lilies. For me, I realize.

Tomorrow is the day of all Souls. I will see Lilian in Hell, but I never want to see Abraham again.

IMPROVISE

Dr. Kuehler contemplated the options presented by his workshop. His assistant, the ambitious Fred Osborn, waited nearby. Two young bodies, a male and female, lay stabilized on a slab beneath a sheet. Kuehler had surreptitiously recovered them from a traffic accident before emergency personnel arrived. Now, they clung to the thin membrane between life and death.

"Brain transplant?" Kuehler suggested. "It would certainly lead to some interesting experiments regarding human sexuality."

"If I may be so bold sir, the damage caused to the male compromises the validity of that endeavor."

"Hmm. Then improvise. Produce something marvelous."

"I won't disappoint you."

SHATTERED

Joe walked into the antiques shop still riding a wave of elation that had only begun to crest. The shop had a narrow storefront in Chinatown, a bright red and gold dragon flying at the top of its sign, proclaiming the little store *Lost Generations of Qing and Ming*. As the wooden door clattered shut behind him with a tinkle of bells, a young woman sitting behind the counter looked up and gave him a polite smile. She sat next to a much older woman, one aged enough to be her grandmother, a possibility more likely that not considering they both had brown eyes peering through glasses that rested on dimpled cheeks. "Let us know if there's anything we can help you find," the young woman said. Joe nodded, and flashed a grin. The girl looked back down at a tablet resting on the counter and continued to scroll. The older woman gave him a moment's glance, and then sipped from a steaming tea cup.

He walked slowly through the aisles of antiques and curiosities, running his fingers along ceramic statues, gazing at scrolls and paintings even older than the white haired woman sitting behind the counter, but in his mind the *Payments Received* screen of his Paypal account was all that he could see.

Last night, Joe had published a new post for *E-Crack*, a website that promised "the internet's most addictive content". As a free-lance writer, he spent a few hours each day writing click-bait for different websites, much of it "sponsored content", a tortured euphemism that described what amounted to digital ad-copy for whoever paid for it. But he liked *E-Crack*, because it was pure silliness and entertainment. Nobody came there to decide which smartphone to buy.

Until this morning, writing for these kinds of websites had been like panning for gold. He might get a few thousand hits and shares, enough for the site to pay him a few hundred dollars from time to time, but not much more than would help him scrape by with the expenses he shared with his girlfriend, living crowded with their cat in a Williamsburg studio. Today when he'd woken up, he checked the revenue generated by his most recent post, a series of fake text conversations among history's world leaders, living and dead. Imagining the texting habits of Joan of Arc and Genghis Khan had struck a chord. He'd even ascribed them personalities: the Khan was a meat-headed 'bro', while Joan was an artistic eccentric who insisted she found inspiration from the voices in her head she swore were real. The post generated $24,681.72 for him in less than twelve hours. From the time he made the post, went to sleep, and woke up, he'd earned more for himself than he had in the entire past year.

For a moment, he thought someone must be playing a prank on him, or perhaps his Paypal account had been hacked to hide or launder money. In a few moments, the fortune might transform into a pile of bitcoins for a Russian oligarch. But no, *E-Crack* listed 1.4 million views for the post, 600k shares on Facebook alone. Other websites were writing about the post and linking to it, creating an avalanche of traffic to *E-Crack* which hadn't peaked until mid-morning.

He'd remembered to check his phone then. Twenty-six missed calls. They started about three hours after he'd made the post. The summer's biggest hit-maker, a brand-new, baby-faced rapper, had tweeted a link to it. By the time the East coast had gotten out of bed, the post had already gone viral.

"Mr. Damici," the lead content editor from *E-Crack*, Jane Willowsby, greeted him when he returned her calls. "Joseph. Congratulations. You've generated over a million hits in less than twenty-four hours. And aside from some headaches for our network engineers, everyone's very happy with you. How would you like a position as a full-time content generator? A regular column, whatever you'd like. Three or four posts a week, five hundreds words or less. We need to keep those tasty morsels bite-sized."

"Absolutely," was all Joe could say. With a dry mouth he agreed to a $100k annual salary, with a 1.5% stake in the ad revenue for traffic generated by his articles. And that was it. In a daze, he left his studio with his debit card, and took the subway into Chinatown. He didn't know exactly why, but he felt it would be a good place to spend a lot of money, to buy something unique and useless that would impress his bohemian girlfriend and all their hipster friends. So he'd walked into Qing and Ming. *Four and a half stars on NYSeeit has to mean something, right?*

Joe found a jade dragon sculpted into a candle-stick atop a cylindrical base. The body wrapped itself in a spiral around an absent candle. Its mouth gaped open as if spewing flame; it must create quite an image once the candle's first lit. He examined a laminated card on the edge of the shelf that displayed it. The piece was a 19th century antique from the Qing dynasty, used for writing by candlelight for a scribe or priest. Its price was listed as $400, but for once, blowing half a month's rent on something so frivolous had become inconsequential, so he decided to pick it up.

As he approached the counter, Joe noticed a heavy, wrinkled canvas covering an object resting against the end of an aisle. He pulled a corner of the canvas aside to see a mirror underneath. A smooth sheet of glass shined his reflection back at him. The glass was inside an oval gilded in metal embossed with some kind of writing. Mandarin, if his eyes did not deceive him.

The old woman pointed her finger and hissed words he could not understand. "She says do not touch!" the younger woman translated for him. "The mirror is cursed. Cover it."

Joe complied, but smiled back at them both. "That's good, I like that. You know how to hook a customer. I'll give you a grand for this jade piece and the mirror both."

The older woman frowned. Despite her Mandarin, she understood Joe's words. "You are fool to want that mirror," the older woman spoke in a raspy voice, her accent thick. Her words were clear enough. "It show the truth. Silver inside the mirror will show you spirits. The past, the future. But certain truths not meant to be seen. That mirror drive you mad."

"I get it," Joe chuckled. "I told you, I'll buy the mirror. You trying to drive up the price?"

"That mirror is cursed, sir," the young woman spoke up. "The only reason it's not in our warehouse is because its meant for the junkyard. We received it from an estate sale. The man who owned it threw himself from the roof of his penthouse. He'd lost his wife, his job, half his fortune. Then his life. When we received the mirror, we studied its history. Those words you see around the outside of the pane are black magic. The person who made that mirror was an evil man. Every person who's owned it has been bonded to that mirror until the end of their life. And that end has never been good. Its creator was beheaded after he poisoned the daughter of his provincial governor, along with half their household. The mirror showed him the governor's corruption, and after losing his own infant daughter during a hard winter, burdened with heavy taxes, what he saw through the looking glass broke him. Truth can be a kind of madness sometimes."

"So can refusing a wealthy customer," Joe responded, his tone serious, the grin evaporated. "Do you want my money, or not? This dragon's neat, but I can spend my money elsewhere. And if I can't have the mirror, I don't want the jade either."

"Two thousand," the old woman demanded. "Your fortune turn sour with the mirror, but if you want a curse, I not stop you. You pay for the privilege." The old woman cackled. Her smile was brown from the tea, but her eye teeth were still sharp as daggers.

Joe grunted an affirmative, but the woman's words took some of the fun out of his purchase. The young woman swiped his card with a device connected to her tablet, and turned it around for Joe to sign on the touch screen. He rubbed his finger on its smooth surface, hit the accept button, and turned toward the mirror. "You have something to wrap the canvas with?"

"I give you a rope to tie around the mirror," the old woman said. "Maybe you hang yourself with it."

* * * * *

Joe walked off the elevator into the fourth floor of his apartment building. He held the mirror with both hands, still wrapped in its canvas and tied with the rope. The jade dragon was inside a reusable canvas shopping bag more suited for groceries than priceless relics; it was by far the most expensive item the bag had ever held. By far, the most indulgent. *But I earned this indulgence,* Joe told himself. He approached his studio, leaned the mirror against the wall, yanked his keychain from his jeans pocket, unlocked the door, and walked inside.

His girlfriend, Kat (short for Katarina, but her only her parents called her that), was cooking lunch on their stove. A couple paninis sizzled in a cast iron skillet, some kale with garlic frying in a pot nearby. She had ear-buds in, and washed a few dishes while the food cooked.

"Hey," Joe said to her as he tapped her on the shoulder. Kat's eyes widened for a moment in surprise, but she smiled when she saw him.

"Ha!" she said as she paused her music and unplugged her ears. "Got lost in the suds. You scared the *shit* out of me. Where've you been? Go out somewhere to write?"

"Mm-mm," Joe said. "I went on a little shopping spree, to celebrate. Come here, I want to show you what I got."

Kat turned off the stove, and followed Joe into the front of the studio. He set his bag on the kitchen table on his way out. Joe crouched down, pulled the mirror up, and brought it into the apartment, kicking the door closed on his way in, and gently placing the mirror on their futon. "Here," Kat offered him a serrated steak-knife from their silverware drawer. Joe used the knife to rip through the rope, and the canvas fell open.

"*Dayumn...*" Kat said. "Looks tight. Hey, I know you struck gold with that last post, but let's make this the last reckless purchase for a little while, huh? Our student loans haven't gone anywhere, ya know."

"I know, I know. But let's enjoy this," Joe and Kat stared back at each other in the mirror. Joe smiled. Kat blew up her cheeks like a puffer-fish, and Joe jostled her with his elbow. She smiled and kissed his cheek.

"What's that writing around the mirror?" Kat asked.

"Mandarin. You'll never believe what the old lady at *Qing and Ming* told me about it. She said the mirror's cursed. That it would show me the truth, whether I wanted to see it or not."

Kat's brow furrowed. "Joe, that's creepy. Don't tell me that. I spent half my childhood with the heebie-jeebies, feeling haunted in my bedroom. Nightmares, shadows without light. Don't bring me back into that."

Joe scoffed. "Calm down, Kat. They were just driving up the price. Probably hoping to sell it to somebody with a hard-on for ghost-hunting." Joe saw something flash out of the corner of his eye. "Is Phil here?"

"No..." Kat drew the syllable out. "We're meeting him and Mika for dinner, remember? Nobody's here but us. C'mon, we had some paninis that didn't sell. I cooked 'em for us, and picked some rooftop kale to go with it. You hungry?"

"Yeah," Joe nodded. He gave the mirror a sideways glance, and felt something sink in the pit of his stomach as the old lady's words echoed through his mind. *Enough. You're psyching yourself out.* He *was* hungry, though. So was Kat. They ate quietly for a few moments, taking big bites out of their paninis as olive oil ran down their fingers. Brown paper towels became napkins. Ice-water tinkled in a couple of mason jars.

"Quit looking at it, Joe. You're freaking me out. It's just a mirror, right? We can still chuck it out if we need to. Just don't tell me how much you paid for it if we do," she said with a wink.

Joe pulled his eyes from the mirror. Even though he'd looked at it sideways, he still had some kind of strange vision when he peered at its surface. He saw Kat (different hair-cut and clothes, but still same ol' Kat) kissing Phil, one of his very best friends. And not in an even remotely platonic way, but part of one of those steamy make-out sessions that usually act as a prelude to sex.

All three had spent their years at CUNY together. *Are they having an affair? She definitely isn't acting like it. But anybody who could get away with something like that for any length of time would have to be good at lying. I need to keep an eye on them at dinner tonight*, he thought, stewing in his imagination.

"Joe!" Kat said, waving a hand in his face. "You've got a thousand-yard stare. Did you see something else when you went out earlier? Something that upset you?"

He flashed a grimace, struggling to transform it into a grin. "No, no. Just have some things running through my head about *E-Crack*. Ideas for posts, things like that."

Kat sighed. "You want your notebook?" she asked. "If these ideas aren't worth writing down, they're not worth taking up our time together."

"No," Joe shook his head. "You're right. Can't become obsessed, or I'm going to burn myself out."

"You done with lunch?" she asked. He nodded. Most of his food was gone, but an edge of his Panini and a few leaves of kale remained. Kat scraped the rubbish into a compost bin, and rinsed the dishes in the sink.

Joe threw the canvas back over the mirror. He was done looking at it for now. Kat gave him a questioning glance.

"'Til we figure out what to do with it. Hey, I almost forgot. I got something else, just for you. A dragon from the east."

* * * * *

El Taqueria bustled with a pleasant buzz of conversation, glass bottles, sizzling fajitas, and Mexican folk music. Joe and Kat sat on one side of a table. Mika and Phil, their closest "friend couple" sat across from them. Together, the pair owned a coffee house that Kat helped them manage.

"To the digital age," Phil raised his *cerveza* and they clinked their bottles together, each taking a sip before setting their bottles back down.

"Thanks for dinner, Joe," Mika said. "How's it feel to strike it rich?"

"Don't think it's sunk in yet," he replied. "Hoping my luck holds out. *E-Crack* is a big name, but who knows how long they'll want me? My contract is for one year. I may be able to turn it into a career. Might just be able to pay off our student loans and save a little nest egg. We'll see."

Kat chuckled. "Lighten up, Mr. Practicality. You know how you're *supposed* to answer that question? 'Well, after becoming the world's most well-known internet writer, I'll launch a humor podcast, and begin building my digital media empire'. So next time, *that's* what you should say."

"If I want everyone to think I'm an asshole," Joe smirked. "No, I get it. I'm lucky. I also have some measure of talent. And I've worked hard to get where I am. I just don't want to make any big plans yet. In case it all comes crumbling down around me, I still want a shred of dignity."

Phil spoke next. "I understand you, man. It's how I feel about the coffee shop. We've been making money for two years, but tastes could change in a couple more, and there's no way to know how well we'd be able to adapt."

"You'd do just fine," Kat replied. *Not a moment's hesitation,* Joe thought. Her eye seemed to shine a bit too bright at that moment. Phil's cheeks looked a shade too rosy.

"Here's hoping," Mika sighed. "Okay, enough doom and gloom. We're here to celebrate. What does everybody want to eat?"

In ten minutes, the server set down bowls of guacamole and salsa that they shared with a basket of warm tortilla chips. Joe also ordered a platter of tacos for them, but otherwise they filled up on beer and appetizers.

The fried tortillas cracked in his mouth, salty and delicious. Piped in Mariachi music provided a soundtrack for people-watching. But Joe still couldn't shake the lingering doubt and suspicion from the vision he'd seen in the mirror. Kat and Phil sat diagonally from each other, but dominated much of the conversation. Usually, that would be no problem. Joe was good with words, but had more practice writing than speaking. Mika was a slight introvert too, and aside from a few words every now and then, was pleased to have Phil speak more than she did.

In his mind's eye, Joe saw Kat and Phil kissing. Easier now that they were face to face in the restaurant.

"You alright, dude?" Phil asked. "Looks like you're about to lose it."

Joe flashed a quick grin. He realized his knuckles were white. A half inch of beer warmed in the bottom of his bottle. He drained it. "You know," he said, pointing to his head and making a circle in the air. "It goes where it wants to."

"Damn, Joe, you need to chill the fuck out," Kat admonished. "Hey, there's an alley behind this place. Real chill, it's where the workers go to on their smoke breaks. Wanna sneak back there? If you give me your card, I can pay the bill, and we can torch this joint Johnny gave me." Johnny had a medical card. He'd moved on from the coffee shop, but traded his extra smoke for bags of coffee from Kat and the others.

"Yeah," Joe said with a bit more ice in his voice than he intended. Three pairs of eyes stared at him. "Didn't realize success would bring this much stress," he sighed. "Thanks, Kat," he handed her his debit card. "We'll meet you outside."

* * * * *

The smoke helped a bit. Joe felt a slight calm as he exhaled from his nose, and passed the nickel-sized roach to Phil. A few stars were visible. They peeked through the gaps between buildings. Even in one of the brightest cities in the world, some stars could still shine through. A few pigeons ruffled through trash piled in the alley. *Koo-oo-o, koo-oo-o.* "They're talking to us," Joe said. "Eating our left-overs."

Kat smiled and kissed his cheek. Warmth spread from her lips to his chest and out to his fingers. He felt connected to everything around him. Not only his friends, but the pigeons in the alley, the stars above him, even the brick wall he leaned against.

A door opened from the back of the restaurant. A cook was hauling a full bag of garbage and threw it into the dumpster. Mika was startled for a moment, and hid the joint behind her back. "Relax," Phil chuckled as he spoke. "Dude works at a restaurant. He's gotta be cool. Hey, amigo!" he called out. "You wanna finish this?"

The man smiled. He wore jeans, a black tee-shirt, and a ball cap over his head. His voice had a thick accent. "Gracias," he said. He wiped his fingers on his jeans and took the roach. He smoked until it burned his fingers, and flicked the remnants back into the alley. "Back to work. Very busy. Thank you, thank you," he said as he walked back inside.

"Alright. You guys wanna head to a bar? Keep celebrating?" Phil asked.

"They might want some time with each other," Mika told him. "Not sure I have a 'party 'til dawn' night left in these old bones, anyway."

"Yeah, think we're gonna go *home* and keep celebrating," Kat told them. "You ready to head back, Joe?"

"Yeah, let's go. I'm ready to take it easy." Joe came to Phil and gave him a tight hug. A little too tight. Phil grunted an *oof* before Joe let go. He hugged Mika too, as Phil and Kat shared their own friendly squeeze.

* * * * *

Fifteen minutes later, Kat leaned her head against Joe's shoulder as they rode the subway back to their neighborhood. Kat dozed, and Joe glanced at their reflection in the widow. The *shuhshushshush* of the train was hypnotic. Joe rode his buzz all the way home. And even though the window wasn't a mirror, the reflection it cast was comforting. It showed him the truth he *did* want to see. All else remained hidden beneath the *shush* of the subway and the head on his shoulder.

He nudged Kat when they came to their stop. She shook off her nap, and walked with him out the train's door and up the subway steps to the surface. In a couple blocks, they were back at their building, walking through the doors together, taking the same elevator Joe had brought the mirror and the jade dragon up in. Kat had her key ready, and let them both in.

She walked into their kitchen, pulled open the fridge and leaned inside. "We have a little less than half a bottle left. Wanna help me finish it?"

"Yeah," Joe said. "Bring it out. I'll get a couple glasses." He placed the wineglasses next to the jade dragon candlestick. Earlier, Kat found a candle that was the perfect width and they'd cut it to the correct length to reach the dragon's maw. Joe flicked his lighter and gave the jade dragon its fiery breath. Kat turned off the kitchen light, and giggled as they stood together in the candle-light.

"Thanks, Joey," she spoke softly as she poured a bit of wine into both glasses.

They brought their glasses over to their coffee table, and set them down. Joe moved the mirror from the couch and leaned it against the wall with the canvas draped over it. He slumped down into the cushions and wrapped his arm around Kat's shoulder. She leaned her body into his and took a sip of wine, then cradled the glass against her body. In the small space of the studio, the candle cast a soft glow that filled the apartment with a dim light.

A soft rustle came from the canvas as it slumped to the floor. Joe's eyes darted to the mirror. It was a reflex, alerting him to the source of an unfamiliar noise, but he could see into the glass and what it revealed hurt him deeply. Kat and Phil were wrapped around each other, bodies entwined, faces wound tight in masks of ecstasy, their bed rocking rhythmically. *Something doesn't add up. Is this mirror tricking me? I've never seen that room. Not in our studio, not in Phil's apartment either. And they look so different in the mirror. Not like they do today. What the hell is going on?*

Kat felt Joe tense. She set her wine glass on the coffee table and turned to him. "Relax, Joey…" she ran a few fingers through his hair. "What's going through your mind?"

He breathed a heavy sigh. His fingers laced together, wrapped around the wine glass. "Are you and Phil having an affair?"

"Jesus Christ, Joe," Kat said, anger in her voice. She set her glass down. "Of course not. He and his girlfriend are my *bosses*. You really think I would be that stupid? Where is this *coming* from? You're not even the jealous type…"

"It's coming from that god-damned mirror," Joe seethed. "And the words that old shop-keeper said to me. That the mirror would show me truths I wouldn't want to see. Well, I certainly don't want to see what that mirror's showing me now. Know *you* can't see it. You're not the mirror's owner. I see you and Phil…" his voice began to choke. "I see you *fucking*. Your hair looks shorter than it is now, and it's a bedroom I've never seen before. But I know it's you. And I know it's him."

"You know I'd never do that to you, Joey," Kat told him. "I love you, I don't even want Phil."

"So why I am seeing that in the mirror?!" Joe snapped. "It wouldn't *show* me that for no reason. Either *I'm* insane, or that curse is real. The mirror is showing me a truth I don't want to see, and I can't think of seeing *any*thing more painful than my best friend and my lover tangled up in bed together."

Kat sighed. "I don't think you're crazy. I think that mirror's showing you a window into the past." She'd put her wine glass down too, and slumped forward with her head in her hands.

"The past?" Joe's eyes narrowed as he asked. "You and Phil had sex and neither of you ever *told* me?"

"We weren't officially a couple back then. Yeah, we'd gone out a couple times. Even fooled around a little. But we weren't exclusive. At least...I wasn't. Phil and I were at the same party that night. Think you were visiting your parents. Anyway. We went home together. And once you and I became an item, Phil told me we shouldn't ever tell you, and I agreed."

"You agreed to lie to me," Joe told her, tears in his eyes.

"Joe, I'm so sorry. We never meant to hurt you. But we weren't even a couple back then. I was getting to know both of you. We were safe. It happened once. It was years ago," Kat explained.

Joe walked to the kitchen table. He picked up the jade candlestick. He looked at Kat. She cowered against the couch, afraid he was about to fling the object at her. Instead, he turned to the mirror and hurled it at the glass pane with all his force. The mirror shattered, and the world turned red.

* * * * *

Detective Corrigan studied the pooled and dried blood on the studio floor. Bits of clothes, bones and hair were scattered nearby. The forensics team crouched close to the mess, collecting a bizarre smattering of evidence that had been left behind. Corrigan, a homicide detective, led the investigation, but didn't know yet what to make of it.

A downstairs neighbor brought the incident to the attention of the police. Blood had leaked from her ceiling. When the police entered, a young woman had been found clutching her cat, sprayed in the blood of the deceased. Whether he was the victim of a crime or an accident, Corrigan had yet to determine. The woman was still in a state of deep trauma, now in psychiatric treatment at a Brooklyn General Hospital. Her cat, much to the chagrin of the investigators, had escaped the studio or hidden itself so well nobody had been able to find it. All that remained in the studio now was the remnants of the body and all the couple's possessions.

"Any theories, Ms. Williams?" Corrigan asked. Williams was crouched on the floor, her gloved hands tucking a hair sample into a zip-locked bag.

"Not yet," she said rising. "We've ruled out explosives due to the lack of any kind of residual damage to the area surrounding the body. No noise reported either, except from the woman's screams. I'm stumped. Never seen injuries like this before."

"Me neither," Corrigan admitted. "Hell of a body to catch."

"Any suspects yet?" Williams asked.

"Only the woman. Katarina Popov, known as Kat. Been living with the deceased for a few years, but once we calm her down and question her, I doubt we'll be able to come up with any hard evidence. If she'd done it, I think it'd be a bit more obvious. No weapon, no motive beyond your usual romantic bumps in the road. But hell if I know who else it'd be."

Williams' eyes glimmered as a new idea flashed in her mind. "You know, about fifteen years ago, I got called to a scene that reminds me of this. At least a little bit. Industrial accident. A tank of liquid nitrogen leaked from a broken valve and covered a custodial worker. He fell to the ground, and shattered to pieces. Wasn't found until the next morning. Once the nitrogen was spent and dissipated, his remains thawed. Looked a little something like this."

Corrigan nodded. "Shattered. That's a good word for it. Shattered and melted into bloody goop." He looked around the studio, hoping to see something that would give him an idea. "Hey, Williams," he said, pointing to an object leaning against one of the walls. "Wasn't there a crack in that mirror when we walked in here?"

Williams followed his eyes. "I remember a spider-web of cracks in that glass, from some kind of impact. But you're right, doesn't look damaged anymore."

"That *is* weird," Corrigan remarked. "Well, let's close up the scene. If the next of kin claim the possessions, that mirror will be theirs. It'll be someone else's problem."

PART III

CYCLE OF THE SEASONS

That which hath been is now; and that which is to be hath already been; and God requireth that which is past.

-Ecclesiastes Chapter 3, Verse 15, King James Version

I should have loved a Thunderbird instead;
At least when spring comes they roar back again.
I shut my eyes and all the world drops dead.
(I think I made you up inside my head).

-From "Mad Girl's Love Song" by Sylvia Plath

SPRING

Violet Bloom
Violet bloom
By the silent tomb

Gentle kicks
In a widow's womb

Raindrop tears
Are all she hears

Her heart beats
Through the gloom

The Muddled Pain of Maybes
Mud and blood
Pollen and flood

Puddles, eggs and babies

Fear not the thunder
Nor hearts torn asunder

From the muddled pain of 'maybes'

Summer

A pair of haikus by John Beechem (L) and Thomas Beechem (R)

The cicada cries	Seventeen year pulse
In the heat of the day star	Bookmarks of a novella
Sweat drops like a tear	Marking my epochs

Autumn

Fall Ramblings
Fall is a feathered forest of fire
Empty chlorophyll facsimiles
Paint Mother Nature
Sidewalk chalk

Albino squirrels whose
Pink eyes
Trick and treat themselves
To green iron trash cans

Orange moons in Jefferson County
And Pink Floyd from funky speakers
Under a carpet of stars
As thick as my hair

Neon post-it notes hugging
Stout stone giants
Among teeth like waves
Holding my bicycle

A billboard near a bridge
Where Barbara Bush cleans
Windows in a dress of bright blue
Hideousness, pearls old ladies wear

Grandmother sentry with a smile of hemlock

WINTER

A Song for Winter
Beneath the roots of the Yggdrasil tree
A chipmunk dreams of spring
But deaf to the chirps of the robin's plea
Only the cold winds sing

Odin sleeps in a vast stone hall
And waits for the sun's return
While shadows grow and black gloom falls
Slowly, the Earth does turn

On craggy peaks, frost giants tread
In the valley, dishes rattle
A mother mourns, her babe is dead
The sound of a silent rattle

'Do not despair!' the faerie cry
'Warmth is on its way'
They wipe the tears of the lady's eye
And let her sleep the pain away

With berry red and holly green
Evil kept at bay
All through winter's longest night
We shall wait the day

PART IV

SECRETS OF THIS CORE

My brain is only a receiver, in the Universe there is a core from which we obtain knowledge, strength and inspiration. I have not penetrated into the secrets of this core, but I know that it exists.

-Nikola Tesla

In order to rise from its own ashes, a Phoenix first must burn.

-Octavia Butler

ILLEGAL ALIENS

Xander looked out from the pilot's seat of his craft, and saw the blue orb of Earth glowing in the darkness of space. It was a good view, and from his perspective he could make out the coast of California against the Pacific Ocean, as his eyes followed the coastline north until it reached Alaska, obscured by swirling white clouds. His two long fingers cradled a bottle of beer against his thumb, and he brought it to his lips to drink.

"You're drifting to port," his companion, Zeek, told him.

Xander looked at his co-pilot through a haze of cigarette smoke, and nodded. He used his left hand (the one not holding the beer) to correct the ship's course and become level with the Earth's upper atmosphere. Xander had been skimming the stratosphere as he made his way around the northern hemisphere, watching the clouds swirl and looking for thunderstorms to watch. The pattern of the ship's movements made a graceful figure eight between the earth and the moon, using the planet's gravity to pull it around the Earth's northern hemisphere before the ship's momentum flung it like a slingshot towards the moon. He circled around the dark side of the moon, piloting the craft back toward Earth to begin the cycle again.

Zeek looked at the radar screen, and thought about how the ship's graceful circuit was like the minuet of an Andromedan star dancer, gliding through the vacuum of space as smoothly as a dancer's feet against a polished floor. He began to trace the craft's path using the cigarette he held in his right hand to orbit his left fist. His blank black eyes reflected the glowing tip of his cigarette, and he took another drag after a few more moments of tracing the ship's pattern.

The radio switched from Perry Como to Frank Sinatra, and Xander increased the volume. Zeek hummed the melody as Xander tapped the drum beat out on the ship's control panel. The music attracted them to the planet first, reaching them on their radio as they navigated the asteroid belt one night looking for a good place to hide out from the Galactic Bureau of Investigation. The GBI had pursued them past Alpha Centuri trying to catch up with the craft, an exploration saucer used by the inhabitants of the Milky Way's Gamma Quadrant. It was a fast craft, powered by a hydrogen fusion reactor encased in the ship's core. The ship itself was shaped like a round disc that orbited a central command center. The command center was slightly raised with window screens that looked out 360 degrees from the ship. As the outer disc spun around the craft, the console of the command center faced the direction the ship travelled. The two were connected by powerful magnets that kept the parts together without them ever actually coming into contact.

The plan to hide in Earth's solar system had worked well. The millions of asteroids in the belt between Mars and Jupiter could hide their ship easily, and despite the GBI's best efforts to find them, Zeek's improvised cloaking device made detection by conventional means next to impossible. They remained in the belt for about a week, but instead of travelling to a nearby star system to sell the stolen craft, they remained near Earth. The siren call of jazz and other popular music anchored them to the blue planet, the radio waves of earth's music stations reaching the craft mere seconds after they left their source. Zeek had even found a way to change the primitive television waves coming up from the planet into images that were projected on the large communication screen usually used to communicate to other ships and star-ports. Instead, it showed Joe DiMaggio batting for the New York Yankees in Yankee Stadium. Other times, it showed a family sitting around a table sharing a meal. Strange, disembodied laughter punctuated the conversation, and Zeek and Xander eventually realized this indicated the punch-lines of jokes.

Xander hummed along with Sinatra's crooning as he drained the rest of his beer. He went back to a small refrigerator the two had scavenged from an abandoned apartment in El Paso, Texas, pulling the handle on the box until it opened and cool steam leaked out into the ship's cabin. A bottle opener was attached to the side of the fridge, and Xander popped the lid off into a pile of red caps that littered the floor. He turned to walk toward the view screen just as an enormous object collided with the ship's massive window. A thin crack appeared and spread ten feet across the location of impact.

"Zeek, give me a status report," Xander commanded.

"Aye, Captain. Minor damage to the view window, but she should hold up on re-entry. Scanning other systems."

"Why didn't the object show up on our radar?"

"Too small, sir. It was a tiny asteroid our sensors were unable to detect.

"Damn our luck."

"Yes, sir."

"Hmm. Run a diagnostic scan. Let's make sure she's not too damaged."

A few moments later, the ship listed hard to starboard, and Xander stumbled drunkenly to a railing. As he fought back a wave of nausea, an alarm sounded and the cabin turned red with the glow of the emergency lights.

"Status!" Xander demanded.

"Major damage to the hydrogen core, Captain! Too deep to detect during the initial scan."

"Initiate emergency landing procedures. Head to coordinates 6-15-22. It's the site of a recent nuclear weapons experiment. Perhaps we can confiscate some leftover plutonium, and use it to fuel our trip away from this solar system. It's going to be a rough, landing Zeek. I'll try to hold her together as best I can."

* * * * *

Andrew McGilicutty peered from his window after hearing a booming thud outside his modest home. In the distance, he saw a pillar of smoke rising from the ground near a corral on the far side of his ranch. Andrew wrapped a towel around the handle of a cast iron skillet he was using to fry a couple eggs, and moved it from the stove. He took his heavy coat off the back of the chair it was resting on, pulled the brim of a worn baseball cap over his brow, picked up a rifle and went outside to investigate.

The red, baked soil of the ranch crunched under his feet as he walked toward a pillar of smoke rising from the east. The sun had just begun peeking out over the horizon and Andrew pulled the brim of his cap down to keep the light from blinding his eyes. He walked past a cattle pen, and noticed the bulls and cows were nervous, pacing around the fence and looking up at him with questioning eyes. Andrew shifted the rifle in his hands, gripping the butt and the barrel nervously. As he approached the source of the smoke, he walked up the lip of a giant crater that had formed. The loose sand of its rim collapsed under the weight of his boots as he marched past it and looked down into a hazy pit.

A strange, shimmering metal monstrosity lay in its center, broken and burning. Andrew slowly descended into the large crater, walking sideways down its rim, displaced soil rolling down in tiny cascades. As he approached the burning hulk, he felt heat from the fiery wreckage on his face. Peering into what looked like massive metal plates that had been shed from a central frame, Andrew noticed an oozing black puddle. He used the barrel of his gun to pry one of the plates up from where it had landed, and recoiled at the site of a long, gray arm with what looked like a three fingered hand on the end of it.

Andrew quickly backed up, nearly tripping over a bit of debris strewn behind him. The hand started moving, and pushed up against the metal plate that was on top of it. Andrew picked up the sheet of metal, planting his feet and pushing it off whatever was trapped beneath it. Underneath, a strange gray being with thin arms and legs, about six feet long, looked up at him. Its other hand was clutching a large bruise on its side, and with pleading black eyes inside an oval shaped smooth face, the creature asked for "A little help, please?"

Andrew put down his gun, then crouched and lifted the strange being up from the ground. He placed his right arm around its waist, and put one of its arms around his shoulders. Andrew pulled the being up to the rim of the crater as it walked alongside him. Once they'd reached the top of the crater, the being pointed back to the wreckage and rasped, "My friend..." Andrew placed him gently against the outer rim of the crater and walked back down to the wreckage.

He pulled up the large, metal plates one by one. Strange instruments that looked like gleaming buttons and radio dials were attached to some of the metal plates, deeper inside whatever it was that Andrew had found. He found a hand and arm clutching what looked like a lever. Pulling a strange metal instrument up from the floor, he found an unconscious being underneath, nearly identical in appearance to its companion. Andrew had helped wounded men during the war, and took the being out of its craft without even thinking. He threw the alien's body over his shoulders as he would a sack of potatoes, and climbed back out of the pit.

"Thank you," the first figure said in a strange accent Andrew couldn't place. "My name is Xander. This is my accomplice, Zeek."

"Andrew McGillicutty, much obliged," he said as he stretched out his hand.

Xander recognized the Earth custom from a few movies and put his hand out in an awkward greeting. He gripped Andrew's large hand in his spindly gray fingers and raised them up and down. Xander noticed that their two bodies were about the same temperature. When he reflected on the implications of this discovery, he realized his chances for survival here were good. Andrew's biology, more or less, mirrored his own, albeit in a crude, primitive way.

He turned toward Zeek, and placed his hand upon his friend's stomach. A bright light emanated from Xander's fingers, and Zeek's stomach also brightened. Slowly, his skin became transparent, and Xander could see the inner workings of his body. He chanted a verse from a song in his native tongue to help him concentrate, as Andrew looked on puzzled.

Their language was foreign to Andrew, and completely unfamiliar. *At least they're not Ruskies*, he thought. When they came out of the wreck, Andrew guessed they must be disfigured, burned beyond recognition or perhaps wearing some kind of skin tight suit that masked their appearance. From what he saw from them now, he slowly began to suspect that these people weren't even human. What to call them then? 'People' implied humanity, but clearly these weren't humans. Yet Xander's actions showed more humanity than some people showed in a lifetime.

Hours wiled away listening to radio shows and reading pulp novels had given Andrew an education in the extra-terrestrial. These people looked like the inhabitants from a strange world encountered by Buck Rogers or battled by Superman in a kid's comic book. How could this be real then? For this to be real, Andrew thought, then he himself must be a character in a pulp novel or a radio story, but that must not be true. He could feel the gun in his palms, squeeze it tightly, feel the warmth of the rising sun on his brow, and know he wasn't dreaming.

"Aliens..." Andrew uttered astonished.

"We are all aliens to someone, Andrew. To us, you are the alien, and this strange world is inhabited with all kinds of freakish creatures compared to our own mundane world."

"I never knew your kind could be so philosophical," Andrew mused.

"There's much you don't know about us, just as there's much we don't know about you. Unfortunately, the cultural exchange between us will have to wait. Zeek is dying, I'm afraid. Perhaps if you have some medical tools I can try to save him, but his chances aren't good."

"Come with me."

* * * * *

Andrew held a kerosene lantern in a room he used to house his veterinary equipment. Usually, it was his place in the barn to birth calves. Every once in a while, he used it to set a broken leg or keep a sick animal away from the others. He'd never used it as an operating room, though that's what Xander was doing now.

Zeek lay on the table unconscious. Xander had cut him open with an instrument he'd salvaged from the wreck, and was using the supplies in Andrew's barn in an effort to keep the procedure as sterile as possible. Andrew marveled at what Xander called a "lazer scapel," a device that emitted an intense beam of light that cut through flesh. "The last time I used this," Xander remarked, "I was recovering a gambling debt from an Andalusian freighter pilot."

Andrew's eyes widened in horror. From what he could tell of

Xander, the alien had a sick sense of humor. He seemed to be good friends with Zeek, but treated him like a business partner as much as a friend, acting in part like he was protecting his investment by trying to save him. After about an hour of cutting, stitching, sponging blood, and even more stitching, Zeeks' wound closed. Andrew admired Xander's skill. He obviously knew a great deal about medicine, enough to confidently perform a complicated procedure. His poise was incredible too. The alien didn't show any signs of stress, or if he did, Andrew didn't know how to detect them.

"I don't think there's much chance for recovery," Xander sighed. "One of his ribs pierced a lung, and I was able to stitch the wound so it could heal. It's unfortunate he's already lost so much blood, because I don't have the equipment for a transfusion."

"You did the best you could," Andrew said, placing the kerosene lamp back on its shelf and turning out the flame. Enough light from the sun pierced through the rafters so the two of them could see their way out of the barn. Rays of light shone through clouds of dust, and as Xander walked through them his smooth gray skin reflected a shiny veneer. The alien walked purposefully, confidently, and somehow without fear. Andrew suspected this hadn't been the first time he had found himself on a strange, possibly hostile planet.

Xander felt a strange sense of calmness. No matter Zeek's outcome, a sense of finality crept over him. He was on a strange, uncharted planet in the outer rim of what was known here as the Milky Way galaxy. If he did manage to make a distress call powerful enough to reach the civilized worlds, it would bring the GBI upon him, and he would spend the rest of his life in prison for his crimes or be executed. On this world, he was a freak, could not pass as a human, and would have to live in isolation or hidden on Andrew's property. Andrew, at least, seemed to be a man of high moral integrity. He suspected the human wouldn't turn him in to local authorities, and even though he lived in isolation, perhaps he'd let Xander stay and help with whatever this land's purpose was.

From what Xander could determine, this place was used to raise strange horned, four-legged beasts that were clearly unintelligent. There were also rows of plants that grew in a predictable pattern, and

Xander recognized this as a primitive kind of agriculture. Whether the horned beasts were raised for labor, food, or both it was obvious they were Andrew's most important possessions. He fretted about the "cattle" as he called them, and told Xander their arrival "spooked" them.

The pair walked back into Andrew's small ranch house. Andrew threw his half cooked eggs out, and placed a half a dozen back into the frying pan after scrambling them in a bowl. Xander sat on one of Andrew's chairs, his feet planted on the floor.

"Do you mind if I turn on the radio?" Xander asked, eyeing a small transistor resting on a shelf in the kitchen.

"No, go right ahead," Andrew responded.

Xander turned it on and scanned the airwaves for a good signal. Eventually, he settled on a jazz station and the music played softly in the background, loud enough to hear but quiet enough to let the two carry on a conversation.

"I must thank you for your hospitality, Andrew. I regret to inform you our arrival here has put you into some level of danger."

"What do you mean? I don't need no trouble. I got enough trouble as it is, keeping up with this ranch."

"There's no reason to be alarmed. But the GBI, excuse me, the "Galactic Bureau of Investigation" might have detected our crash. If they did, they'll send agents here to arrest me. Now that you've helped us, they may consider you an accomplice, aiding and abetting a known criminal."

"Horse puckey," Andrew spat. "I didn't know you were a criminal when you landed, though I had my suspicions before you told me. I guess I'm stuck now. Either way, I won't leave the ranch without a fight."

"You could be incinerated," Xander replied. "Though resistance is most likely the best course of action if they do try to take you. I'd hate to think of what would happen if you were studied and dissected."

"Heh," Andrew said. He thought about a story he heard on the news recently, about the medical experiments the Nazis performed during the war. Nothing could be worse than what those Jews must have gone through, but Andrew didn't want to take his chances with any aliens either.

"Tell me, Xander," Andrew said as he worked the eggs with his spatula, "what kind of criminal are you?"

"An unlucky one," Xander replied.

Andrew chuckled; Xander found it contagious, and began laughing too. *It is incredible how similar our two species are*, Xander thought.

"I was an orphan on my world. My foster parents neglected me, so I ran away as soon as I could. For protection, I joined a street gang. We sold drugs, prostitutes, fought with other gangs, and inevitably died or were arrested. I tired of this chaotic life of violence after a few years, so Zeek and I left the city of our birth, and went into business for ourselves. We started small, breaking into homes, stealing valuables, and then gradually set our sights higher. We hijacked freighters, sold them along with their contents, and eventually stole that exploratory craft that just crashed into your planet."

"With that ship, we could evade almost any local law enforcement, and became more daring. Unfortunately, after a few years of success, Zeek had to kill a GBI agent to make an escape. We fled to the outer rim of this galaxy, the GBI pursued us, but we were able to escape with the help of a cloaking device Zeek constructed. For the last few weeks, we'd been orbiting your planet and its moon, listening to radio, picking up its transmissions, and learning about your culture."

"How could you understand any of it? How come you can speak English?"

"My species has a very advanced verbal capacity. With just a few limited resources, we are able to begin to understand the meanings behind words from inflections in speech, actions, pictures, and words. It happens without us even trying, so after our equipment picked up your transmissions, we knew most of your language in a few days. In fact, we know a few different Earth languages to some extent, but began to use English because we're so fascinated by American culture. The music, the sex, the politics, the blustering arrogance of this nation..."

"You sound like some kind of commie, calling America 'arrogant'.

We aren't full of ourselves. America is top dog. After dubya dubya two, we were the only country in the world with the Bomb. Now it's us against the Ruskies, but I'm done fightin'. That's why I built this little ranch, to get *away* from everybody."

"I didn't mean to offend you, Andrew. Perhaps 'arrogant' was the wrong word to use. Nevertheless, your country does like to throw its weight around, but that's the same as every powerful nation. My own world is just one among millions. To join the Galactic Federation, a world must forsake wars except in cases of self-defense. Aggressive planets are overwhelmed and destroyed by all others. Our weapons are so terrible, war means death for billions. We gave up fighting long ago."

"Hmph," Andrew said. Even though Xander's statements sounded boastful, he had to admit it made him jealous to imagine a planet where no one puts up with war.

With the pop of his toaster, Andrew turned off his stove's burner. He placed a meal of scrambled eggs, toast, jam, coffee, and orange juice in front of Xander, and served the same to himself.

"I'm starvin'" Andrew said.

Xander looked at the food and his utensils. He picked a fork, gripped it with his two long fingers and thumb, and began eating. The food was delicious, warm, and full of life. For weeks, Xander and Zeek survived on space rations, food that kept indefinitely, bland though nutritious. Earth food, at least the food Andrew cooked, was full of flavors, fresh, and simple.

"My compliments to the chef," Xander said with a smile.

Andrew grinned. He hadn't heard a compliment, or even had a conversation in months. The pair ate quickly, silently. Xander kept looking out the window nervously, but he couldn't see anybody or anything outside. Andrew sensed Xander's anxiety, but understood he had reason to worry.

Once they finished eating, Xander helped clean up the kitchen. He worried about Zeek, and felt bad that his friend might die because they lingered too long near Earth. As he toweled the dishes dry, Andrew whistled a tune next to him that Xander recognized from the radio.

Once their work was done, the pair went to the barn to check on Zeek.

Andrew pulled a hand-rolled cigarette from his pocket, one he made from a cluster of tobacco plants that grew on the farm. He offered one to Xander who examined it. Andrew struck a match on a pair of jeans and lit his own, offering the match to Xander who puffed on it until it lit.

"Mmm...crude, but delicious," Xander said.

"Thank you," Andrew replied. "They got cigarettes where you come from?"

"Yes, we do. Actually, our scientists have created a plant that contains nicotine, but releases no other toxins when it is burned."

"It's a strange galaxy," Andrew remarked, echoing Buck Rogers.

The pair reached the barn, trailing smoke as they entered. Zeek lay on the table. Xander approached, and placed his hand on Zeek's head. Zeek's eyes focused in awareness, and he looked at Xander.

"You..." Zeek said.

"Shh..." Xander quieted him.

"You...I thought you would be dead before me. I always...tried to...play it safe."

"Don't worry. You'll be remembered. I'll build a monument for you on this obscure rock we've found. It will say 'Here lies Zeek, outlaw, genius.'"

Zeek smiled, but didn't reply. Andrew had seen this many times. As soon as a dying man became comfortable, he gave up the ghost and there was nothing left. Xander must have known this, because he placed his fingers on Zeek's forehead, said what sounded like a prayer in his native language, and turned to Andrew.

"Thank you, Andrew. If it's okay with you, I'll need your help burying the wreck. The craft is beyond repair, but I don't want anyone on this world finding it."

"I'll help you," Andrew said. He felt happy. For the first time since the end of the war, he'd felt companionship, brotherhood, even if it was with a freaky space alien and not another human being. Xander felt much the same way. Aside from Zeek, Andrew was one of the few beings he felt true kinship with.

A loud knock sounded on the barn door. The pair looked at each other in horror. Andrew knew there weren't any other people living nearby. How could anybody else even know how to get here?

"They've come for me," Xander said with dread in his voice, "the GBI. I don't know how they've tracked me, but now they're here."

"Just calm down," Andrew replied. "Let me see who it is."

Andrew opened the door slowly to look outside. As soon as the door was partly open, someone kicked it the rest of the way and five men in army uniforms came in, followed by a man in a dark suit. The soldiers grappled with Xander on the floor and bound his wrists together. Andrew looked up bewildered at the scene taking place in the barn. The man in the dark suit examined Zeek's corpse, and motioned a soldier to him. He whispered something in the soldier's ear, and the soldier nodded, picking up the alien and taking him outside.

The soldiers dragged Xander out of the barn, his head sagging between his shoulders. Before he left, he looked up at Andrew, smiled and winked. Andrew smiled back, confused. Once the soldiers left with the two aliens, the man in the dark suit approached.

"Mr. McGilicutty, what a pleasure it is to meet you. My name is Agent Pearcy, CIA." Pearcy flipped open a badge and then put it back just as Andrew leaned closer to examine it. "Come outside with us."

Andrew followed Agent Pearcy and they walked back toward the crash site. The soldiers were loading their captives into an Army truck that Andrew couldn't see inside. Pearcy quickened his pace so that Andrew had to speed up to keep up with him.

"Mr. McGilicutty, the US Army will remove the wreckage from your ranch, and level this crater. You were the victim of a bizarre Soviet hoax, meant to create paranoia and fear among the American people. These 'aliens' are Soviet spies, disfigured to look like people from outer space. The wreckage you saw was from an experimental Soviet craft designed to look like a flying saucer. These spies are now in our custody, but you must promise me never to speak a word of this incident to anybody."

Andrew listened in awe as Agent Pearcy spun a web of deception so obvious that Andrew could not help but bite his tongue to keep from laughing.

"Have I made myself clear, Mr. McGilicutty?"

Andrew nodded.

"If I see so much as a speck of this incident in the newspapers, we will come back for you. You are now in possession of top secret military information, and if you describe what you've seen this morning to anybody, you will be tried for treason and hung."

"I understand, sir."

"You look like a good man, Mr. McGilicutty. For your service to your country today, Uncle Sam has a gift for you. This is a check from the U.S. Treasury worth $5,000. You can invest this into your ranch, or put it under your mattress, it makes no difference to me. I'm in the business of secrets, and those are more valuable than gold."

Agent Pearcy left without saying another word. He hopped into an Army truck that pulled up alongside them and it sped off, leaving a cloud of red dust in its wake. Andrew shook his head, turned around, and walked toward the cattle pen to feed his livestock. The sun was overhead, and the bulls became cranky without their breakfast.

To yellow fever

1

The moth's wings sounded like shuffling paper, its erratic path around the office's lonely light-bulb clumsy and doomed. Murphy's eyes darted back to it every minute or so. The raindrop clatter of the tele-writer paused for a moment, replaced by the moth's whisper and the soft hum of electricity. He raised one of his eyebrows before returning his focus back to the case notes. If not for the previous twelve hours of steady work, nor the dull monotony of his case, his mind would be as sharp and focused as it usually was. Instead, he gulped the dregs of his coffee, chewing the dry crumb of the grinds before swallowing them down. Next, he took a sheaf of old reports, rolled them into a tight cylinder, and swung at the little pest. It wheeled out of the way, but Murphy caught it in his left hand, and resisted the urge to crush the damn thing. He opened his window, threw the moth out to fly back to the moon, and then cut off his light. In the next second, the scratch of a match, and the dim glow of a beeswax candle. Its sweet scent filled the room. Murphy got back to work.

08/23/36 7:46 P.M. Observed subject enter taxi with unidentified woman: White, mid-20's, red-hair, lipstick, black polka dot dress. Followed taxi to W 125th St. Driver let them out in front of the Apollo. The pair walked hand in hand into the theater. Continued photo-surveillance from inside automobile. The show let out at about 11:00 P.M. Pair walked east on 125th St. for four blocks. Followed on foot. Pair seen entering tenement house at 11:37 P.M. At 12:56 A.M., subject observed exiting tenement house, hair disheveled, tie un-tied, lipstick on collar. He took a moment to collect himself, then hailed a taxi and returned home. Subject believed to

A loud knock interrupted Murphy's rhythm. He muttered a curse and grabbed his gun. "Better not be no god-damned junkies. I've had enough." He opened the door slightly but kept its chain in place.

"Mr. Lee? Could I trouble you for a moment? I know it's terribly late, but I heard the sound of your tele-writer." The voice was crisp, quick. The speaker had an accent. Like the men he heard late at night on the BBC. He'd never met one in person.

"What business you got with me?" Murphy asked through the gap in the door.

"It's about your sister, Mr. Lee. I'm afraid she's gotten herself into rather deep trouble."

Murphy's eyes narrowed, but he pulled the chain and let the man in. Despite the heat, he was wearing a three piece suit and vest, all navy blue, with a black bowler hat. He took off the hat, and beneath it was a long-narrow face with a thin-salt and pepper moustache. The man's hair was black, cut short and neat, gray at the temples. Murphy studied the man's cold green eyes, and realized one of them was made of painted glass. He pretended not to notice.

"Take a seat," Murphy instructed. He pointed to a wooden chair, its cushion green with a wicker-back. Two months ago, he'd found it on a curb, and realized it would make his clients more comfortable than the metal folding chair he'd been using.

"The name's Jacobs. Eli Jacobs. I'm an agent of his Majesty, King George. Secret service." Murphy stood in silence for a few moments. Eli had yet to sit, but stood with his hand out-stretched toward Murphy's folded arms. Murphy was cast in the soft glow of the candle, so Eli could see his light skin, the color of oak. His hair was short, but slightly red, almost burnt. His eyes were brown, and a half dozen light freckles rested on his cheeks. He still looked like a boy, barely a man really, but his eyes were old, his voice a deep bass.

Murphy finally shook the man's hand, and offered him a cigarette. Eli accepted, and the pair sat across from each other, two points of flame and smoke in the candle-light. "Tell me about Dee."

"You mean Diane? Of course," Eli cleared his throat; he was no longer used to smoking and stubbed the cigarette out in an ashtray. "Well, she's gone missing with one of our men from the embassy. Terrible business. She shouldn't even be involved, quite frankly. I'm afraid that's one of Thomas's weaknesses. Thomas Hughes. He's the ambassador's secretary. We can't find him. And I'm afraid he was last seen entering your sister's brothel."

Murphy sat in silence for a few more moments. *Her* brothel. She had inherited it, he knew. Earned it, in fact. And as upset as it made him sometimes, he knew that that brothel had put food in his belly and a roof over his head for many years. His mother and sister had both made quite a living. Murphy couldn't blame them. While they were in the whore business, he had robbed criminals, stealing money from bootleggers with a bandana pulled over his face and a tommy-gun in his hand. But in his mind's eye, he remembered his sister's skin, dark as cocoa, her eyes like amber. Sweaty from sex with a couple twenties stuffed into her bra. That's the way he remembered her. Her eyes mocked him from inside his mind, and he shook his head to free himself from the reverie.

"I haven't seen my sister in two years. She ain't here, if that's what you're wondering."

"Of course not, Mr. Lee. But you see, I'm in a pickle. Mr. Hughes, well, he had in his possession some rather sensitive material. And if that material were to be given to the wrong person, his Majesty's very life could be in danger, and the life of your president too. So what do you say, Murphy? For King and country?" Eli placed a twenty dollar bill on Murphy's desk and slid it over. Murphy's eyes widened for a moment, but he didn't blink.

"Double that. Then we'll talk."

"Of course!" Eli replied. "Just consider it a down-payment."

Murphy nodded, put on his sweat-stained oxford and began buttoning. He grabbed his shoulder holster, and hid it under his jacket, suddenly realizing why Eli wore his own jacket despite the heat.

"I know a place. Open all night. They've got air-conditioning."

* * * * *

The coffee tasted better in Slim's Diner, but Murphy was getting a caffeine headache. He wished he could go outside to smoke some reefer and take the edge off, but he'd left it up in his flat. His plate of scrambled eggs and toast sat in front of him, half-eaten.

Eli scraped some maple syrup and pancake crumbs up on his fork and brought them to his mouth, relishing the sweet taste of Americana. He drank milk instead of coffee, but seemed sharper after midnight than most men at noon.

"So you say you haven't seen her or heard from her in two years? And why is that?" Eli asked.

Murphy punched a few buttons on the digi-juke in front of him. Over a thousand songs from the past twenty-five years of popular music, and only a handful were worth listening to. Fats Waller's piano began to tinkle out of the digi-juke's speakers. Murphy closed his eyes to relax for a few moments. He opened them and spoke.

"I was still with the force then. Thought I could use the skills I learned as a boy to earn an honest living. Maybe stay alive past twenty-five. Well, guess I made it." He knocked on the wooden bench of their booth. "Ma had just died. Gave Dee the brothel. Offered me the dope trade, but I didn't want it. Most of those boys had it out for me, anyway."

"Admirable." Eli said. "I'm sure it wasn't easy."

"No, it wasn't. And I knew I looked like an Uncle Tom dressed in blue, but I figured it's better to be locked up by a black cop than a white cop. Better chance of getting to the jailhouse in one piece. Anyway..." he trailed off for a moment as if to collect his thoughts. "I came to the brothel one night off-duty. Only way I ever got to see my sister. Might seem a bit nasty, considering the nature of her business, but I was used to it by then. Least, I thought I was.

"One of the girls pointed me into her office. She usually didn't "work" in that room, if you get my meaning, but my sergeant was inside. Sergeant McCluskey. Getting his shoes shined, so to speak. I don't know why, but when he looked at me and smiled, I pulled him away from her and shoved his night-stick into his groin. And then his mouth. Knocked out two of his teeth and smashed one of his balls. It was a stupid thing to do. I don't think he realized she was my sister. We don't look much alike."

"Had to call in a lot of favors to keep myself alive. Have a contact at the New York Post who threatened to expose the NYPD in a corruption scandal if I were to be harmed. Left the force and began work as a private detective. Been at it for two years. Money's tight sometimes, but I survive. Anyway, I haven't seen or spoken to Dee since that night. Don't figure she misses me much. She hasn't reached out to me either."

"A sad tale," Eli remarked. "Do you have any idea where she might have gone? An old boyfriend, perhaps?"

Murphy chuckled. "Dee had lots of boyfriends. But I know she gave kick-backs to one of the Gambino brothers. The brothel's inside their territory. 'The Brown Bordello' it's called. Terrible name, but my family never showed much class. Anyway, one of the Gambino's boys might tell us something."

"Hmm," Eli pondered. "Won't they be reluctant to give up that kind of information?"

"Way I see it," Murphy explained, "we could try one or two ways. You could use that silver tongue of yours and loosen their lips with a bit of cash. That don't work, I got a Colt .45 should do the trick."

"I like your style, Murphy," Eli said with a grin.

"You boys need anything else?" Their waitress had suddenly appeared, scratching inside the tight spirals of her hair with a pencil.

"Just the check, please." Eli smiled at her pleasantly. Murphy nodded, and she walked away.

"Going to be a dangerous business," Murphy told his new partner. "I need a heavy retainer for this kind of work."

"How about $50 a day plus expenses?" Eli asked.

Again, Murphy's eyes widened. He did his best to stay cool. "Last job paid $75."

Eli rolled his eyes ever so slightly. "$60. His Majesty's not running a charity."

"Deal." They shook hands.

* * * * *

Murphy and Eli stood shoulder to shoulder in the crowded passenger train. It was full of workers on their way to offices, docks and factories, their eyes downcast or scanning one of the morning newspapers. The only sound was the steady hum of the train as it glided over the track. Sunshine filtered through the skyline, pouring into the windows with a shuffling rhythm. Eventually, the train slowed and stopped at one of its platforms, a monument of brick and rust in Striver's Row.

"We need to get off here," Murphy said, and the two men pushed through the crowd and out onto the platform. They took some steep concrete steps down to the street. A vast avenue of row houses, a mix of storefronts and apartment buildings, stretched down the block. Here and there, glowing tele-boards hawked laundry detergent and tobacco, their catchy jingles and shouted slogans assaulting their brains.

"Here we go," Murphy said and pointed to a window glowing with neon letters that read 'Percy's Pawn Shop'. The pair walked up some steps that led into the storefront. Inside the windows hung wooden guitars and brass saxophones. A bell tinkled on the door as Murphy pushed his way inside. Shotguns and rifles hung in a rack behind the counter, and beneath a glass counter, rings, earrings and other jewelry shimmered with a cheap luster.

"Sammy Gambino around?" Murphy asked as the door slammed shut behind him.

A young man with a broad white grin looked up from behind the jewelry. His white and gold shoes rested on the case, legs crossed at the ankles. He leaned back in a rolling office chair, wearing a brown suit and vest. A plump face looked up at them, the rolls of his flesh covering his collar like rye dough. His eyes were bright brown and creamy white, his head shaved bald with the shadow of two day's growth. The man's round mouth opened sleepily. "Who wants to know?" asked a voice soft and lazy.

"Tell 'em it's Lee Murphy with his friend Eli."

"One moment." The man leaned his chair back ever so slightly and opened a white door behind him. "Sammy? It's Dee's brother. He's with a white man." A single grunted syllable came from beyond the door and in a moment, a young man walked out, grinning and surprised.

"Murphy! Long time, no see. Got word from your sister?" Sammy had a slight, muscly chubbiness with bright blue eyes and rosy cheeks. His face was flush and cheerful.

"Naw, I ain't seen her. This is my friend Eli Jacobs. We're lookin' for her. Think she might be in trouble," Murphy explained.

"A pleasure to meet you, good sir," Eli tipped his hat as he shook Sammy's hand.

"Likewise, pop. Look, Murphy, I know you and me had a few run-ins back in the day, but that ain't nothin' no more. Your sister, she ain't paid up. Pretty soon, I got start taking it from her girls, and that never goes smoothly. We might have to rough one or two of 'em up first, and that ain't good for them and it ain't good for business. You help us find your sister, get her money, I'll give you a little piece of the action," Sammy offered.

"You mean you don't know where she is either? That's why we're here," Murphy told him.

Sammy whistled. "Well, shucks fellas, I don't know what to tell you. Seems like we gotta case of a missing whore!" In his thick accent, he pronounced the word '*whoo-ah*'. Murpy grit his teeth but said nothing.

"Ahem," Eli cleared his throat. "Mr. Gambino, has anybody else come into your establishment lately that sounds British? Anybody at all."

"Ooh, you know what, I think Charlie told me something about that," Sammy nodded back to his clerk still leaning in his chair. "But uh, my memory's kinda foggy and you don't want to ask Charlie no questions; he don't like to be disturbed 'cept by customers."

"Laying it on a bit thick are we?" Eli asked as he slipped a folded twenty dollar bill into Sammy's hand.

"We got a young guy, sweatin', nervous, came in here about a week ago. Brought a bunch of old coins, said it was from his grand-dad's collection, real old ones from England. Had a guy named Charles on the head, I said 'How you like that Charlie?' and asked the man what he wanted. Said he needed a gun, couldn't be traced. Couldn't use cash to buy one neither, 'cause his money all had to be accounted for with receipts. Paid extra to make sure it wouldn't be a hassle," Sammy told them.

"Show me your own receipt for the coins," Eli demanded.

"That's gonna cost you, pops," Sammy told him.

"Then let's say we do it for old time's sake," Murphy suggested.

Sammy looked back at Charlie, then at the two men. "Sure, Murphy, sure. Give me a sec." He ducked into his office and came back out in an instant.

"There we go, gentlemen," Sammy showed the pair.

Murphy ripped the page out.

"Hey!" Sammy shouted. Charlie finally leaned forward in his chair and took an interest, but Murphy ignored them both.

"Theodore Huxley. Thomas Hughes?" Murphy asked Eli.

"Certainly," Eli said. "What's that number he left?"

"The three digits after the area code means it's a hotel. Beyond that, we'll need to check the tele-net."

"Very well."

"Sammy, we thank you for your time," Murphy spoke. He folded the torn receipt page and placed it inside his coat pocket.

"Gentlemen," Eli tipped his hat again and nodded. He and Murphy walked out of the store, the door clattering behind them.

Sammy looked at Charlie, his feet back resting on the case.

"Charlie, get my brother on the phone. Think we got a problem."

* * * * *

"Let's go, Murphy. We're not going to get any more information out of him."

"Pencil-necked paper pusher," Murphy grumbled. He and Eli turned and walked from the registration desk. They were able to confirm that a Mr. Theodore Huxley had registered at the Plaza, but he'd requested not to be disturbed, and accepted no calls to his room. Eli attempted to bribe the clerk, but the concierge noticed and threatened to throw them out of the hotel unless they left the registration desk immediately.

"Perhaps if we grab a drink, we'll see him coming in or out. This way, Murphy."

They walked into an extravagant bar-room with a gleaming mahogany bar, high-backed chairs of red velvet, and a robotic wait-staff dressed in white tuxedos. Murphy selected a table with a view of the lobby, and they both took a seat. At once, a server-bot rolled over to them on the bar's electro-grid. Its optic sensors flickered a pleasant green of acknowledgement, and its digitized voice warbled, *"Greetings, gentlemen. What can I get for you?"*

"I'll take a dry martini," Eli said.

"Bourbon. On the rocks," Murphy ordered.

"Certainly. I'll be right back with your drinks," the server-bot told them.

"Hm," Eli said after the bot left, "I see Ford's already released the new models here in the states."

"Glad I picked a profession that hasn't been bot-sourced," Murphy remarked. "Yet."

In a moment, the server-bot returned and gave the men their drinks. With a crackle and a whir, the machine turned and left, navigating a complicated circuit grid that covered the floor of the barroom. The grid glowed a cool wintergreen to match the Plaza's general décor.

"So tell me," Murphy said, "what've you got on this Hughes character? Or I guess I should ask, what's he got on *him* to make a jump across the pond worth it to you?"

Eli arched his eyebrows with a grin and took a small sip from his martini. "The daft fool's gone and taken some classified blueprints, part of the ambassador's air defense briefing. Likely trying to sell them to the highest bidder, and I wager I know who that'll be."

"Not Uncle Sam?" Murphy asked.

"Not for a moment," Eli replied. "Roosevelt's spending too much on public works to be able to feed a war machine. No, I'm afraid he's got his eye on Goering and his *Luftwaffe. Deutchland uber alles*, and all that rubbish. Afraid Hitler's taking the metaphor a bit too literally. Our agents tell us he's already got the map of Europe carved up like mincemeat pie. Only waiting for the right moment to strike."

"Glad he's on the other side of an ocean," Murphy said, taking a stiff drink of his bourbon before setting it back on the table and lighting a cigarette.

"Don't think that'll hold him for too much longer. What I'm about to tell you is strictly top-secret, but I want you to know," Eli explained in a hushed tone, "there's a lot more to this than a rogue diplomat and a missing girl."

Murphy nodded and leaned in. "Lay it on me."

Eli's eyes rose for a moment, then he shook his head dismissively. "Thought I saw him, but the chap was half a foot too short. Anyway. Our engineers have cooked up a design for an aero-plane that can pilot itself and bomb a target thousands of miles from where it lifts off. Can you imagine it? A whole fleet of mindless killing machines, ones that always obey their orders, hitting their targets with computers, then returning to base. Or not. Even if some are shot down, there'd be no more pilots to train, just more machines to push out the factory."

"Sometimes I wonder what kind of world Tesla and Ford have made for us," Murphy sighed. Despite the thousands of conveniences, such as the tele-writers and digi-jukes, just as many weapons had been created, each more deadly than the last.

"It's the one you and I live in," Eli replied coolly, "and I don't plan on leaving any time soon. There's our man."

Eli dropped a bill on the table. Murphy took one last drink from his bourbon, and followed Eli through the lobby. The man looked back; he must have felt eyes on him. Eli hid behind a luggage rack. The man rushed out of the hotel's revolving door.

The door spun until Hughes, Eli and Murphy all stood outside on the crowded street. Hughes broke into a run. So did Eli. Murphy followed sprinting, phlegm rising from his cigarette scorched lungs. He swallowed the bile like a pill, and sped up until he was just behind Eli.

Garbage spilled as their target knocked a trash can into their path and turned the corner down an alley. Eli ran through the rubbish, a scrap of newspaper caught on his chest for a moment on his chest until it flew backward. Murphy batted it away.

A shot rang out, cutting through the air between them. Eli fired two in return, but Murphy ducked behind a metal trash can.

"In the name of King George, lay down your weapon and surrender!" Eli roared, but of course their quarry ignored him.

Murphy stood back up. The boom of his Magnum echoed through

the alley, and Hughes began running again. From the street beyond the alley, they heard the screech of tires.

Eli and Murphy stood panting as the car sped off. "Ain't that a son of a bitch…" Murphy grunted as he holstered his gun.

"Not a complete loss," Eli said. "I recognized that car's plates. They belong to the German Embassy. A bit clumsy to send one after him, but they must have been in a hurry. I suspect Hughes knew we were after him. Perhaps your friend in Harlem has a big mouth."

"Gonna be a lot bigger, I ever see him again," Murphy spoke.

"Ah, here's another taxi. Get in, Murphy. We'll share a cab to Harlem. I've rented a hotel room near you until we end this business. Don't worry about the Germans. I've got a man inside, an attaché. His name's Rudiger. I call him Rudi. One quarter Jew, but the records are forged, so nobody knows. He's a double-agent, the whole reason I know about this damn plot to begin with."

Murphy looked at him with his cool brown eyes. For a moment, Eli thought he would say something, but he only got into the cab and rolled down the window. Murphy told the driver-bot his address, and the car began moving.

2

Murphy had Eli over for breakfast. The heat in the apartment was almost palpable; their only relief came from an electric fan or open refrigerator. Eli scoured the tele-net for information about the German Embassy building as Murphy reviewed his notes on the Gambino brothers. Each man also wore a gun, worried about retribution from Hughes, the Germans, or the Gambinos.

The telephone jingled. Eli picked it up before the second ring. "There's a public telephone just outside," he said by way of answering. "Call me at (101) 757-6300. Give me thirty seconds."

Murphy nodded, and Eli let himself out. There was a brick near the door downstairs Eli used to keep the entryway open.

From the window, Murphy watched the block underneath. Eli was conspicuous, the only white person in sight. He had the smell of a cop on him, Murphy knew, so everybody would keep their distance, at least in daylight. He saw Eli hang up the phone and nod at the window to indicate he was on his way back up.

"He wants to meet us," Eli told Murphy.

"Where?" Murphy asked, buttoning his shirt.

"A coffee shop in Spanish Harlem. Neutral territory, I gather," Eli said.

"Think I know the place," Murphy said. "It's a'ight. I'll lead us there, make sure we're not followed."

They finished dressing, walked down the stairs, and entered the street. Murphy led Eli down into the subway. The cool air was a pleasant relief, but the stink of urine hit them with an acrid tang. Profane graffiti covered the walls and heaps of rubbish were piled here and there. The people on the platform clung to their dignity, at least for the most part.

Eli followed Murphy through the platform, entering one side of a car only to exit from the other before boarding another train completely. They'd switch at the next stop, only to repeat the same trick again. After their third switch, they remained inside their car until the train reached their destination.

Spanish Harlem was just as hot as Murphy's neighborhood, but it sounded different. Eli heard the lilt of Spanish, but not in a Spanish accent. One that he recognized as Caribbean. Mariachi music blared from radios. They passed a bodega and entered a quiet café.

A brown-haired, blue eyed man stood to meet them. "Hello, Eli," he spoke in a German accent.

"Hello, Rudi. Let me introduce you to my partner, Murphy."

Murphy said nothing, but shook Rudi's hand and nodded.

"You're sure you weren't followed?" Murphy asked. He eyed a man in a corner booth reading a newspaper.

"*Ja*," Rudi said. "Have a seat. I ordered us coffee and tea."

Rudi was solidly built, athletic despite his age. He looked to be about as old as Eli, judging from the lines on his face. His eyes were the blue of ice, his jaw hard and square as if cut from granite. He had the face of a movie star, except for a scar that ran from his temple to his chin. With a grin, his features became as soft as a pillow.

"Trench knife," Rudi explained, feeling Murphy's eyes trace down his jaw. "A scratch compared to Eli's wound."

Eli winked his glass eye and the pair chuckled. Murphy looked away and sighed.

"What do you know about Hughes?" Murphy asked impatiently.

"All business. How American," Rudi remarked. "Hughes came to my attention almost a month ago. I intercepted a tele-net transmission to Berlin, promising blue-prints for a new British weapon in exchange for as much cash as it was worth to them. I've found out the damned fool's a degenerate card player. He's up to his ears in debt to the Sicilian mob. Private games. I only know because I was assigned the task to investigate him. I never got a copy of the blueprints, but another agent was able to verify their existence."

"How were you able to learn that?" Eli asked, his left eyebrow raised.

"From another double, one in your agency. I don't know his identity, or you would too, and he'd be dead," Rudi explained. He struck a match and lit a cigarette, using his coffee's saucer for an ashtray.

"No doubt," Eli said. He blew steam from his teacup and sipped Earl Grey.

"Any idea where's he holed up?" Eli asked.

"With the girl, probably," Rudi told him. "He trusts your sister."

"He's a fool," Murphy said.

"What's your plan?" Rudi asked.

"I was hoping *you'd* be able to give us something, some kind of new lead to go on," Eli told him.

"I've one idea, but it's risky. I'd have to blow my cover, so you'll need to get me into England," Rudi explained.

"I guarantee it," Eli promised.

"Good. Let me arrange a meeting with Hughes and the Gambinos. I'll tell him we're going to make the trade," Rudi said. "We'll take him prisoner. Force him to give up the girl."

"Could get messy," Eli said. "I don't like it."

"He'll trust anybody who speaks English with a German accent," Rudi told him. "We're the only friends he has left."

"Tell him to make the drop at the Bordello. I know a few secrets about that place, could come in handy," Murphy said.

"The Gambinos will eat us alive," Eli spoke incredulous.

"If we ask them to make the drop on their turf," Murphy explained, "they'll feel protected. Let their guard down."

"Clumsy," Rudi said. "I like it."

"How do you want to play this, Murphy?" Eli asked.

"I know how to get inside. I can lay a few traps, bring some heat. I know how to fight when I'm outnumbered," Murphy explained.

"His Majesty doesn't want your blood on his hands," Eli said.

"Might be the only way," Rudi offered. "He hasn't handed over the plans yet, but he will soon. The only thing that's kept them out of our hands this long is German bureaucracy. Best to take the initiative."

"Your sister might be hurt, killed," Eli spoke in a hush. "Are you prepared to accept that?"

"She's picked her side," Murphy said. "Lay down with dogs, and all that shit."

"All that shit," Rudi chuckled. "Indeed."

"Then it's decided. Rudi, make the call. We'll begin our preparations."

* * * * *

Murphy crouched on the stone floor of the Bordello's basement. Once, it had been used as a vault to store barrels of booze, but since the end of prohibition, it had been mostly empty. The furnace stood fat and tall, but it was empty too, the space behind its metal grille dark and dusty, full of old, gray coal ash. Once it been his job to keep it stoked in winter, especially around Christmas when half the men in the city were off work and flush with bonuses. His old shovel was even resting against it, the wood pale from where he'd gripped it.

He used a crow-bar to open up a crate of grenades, ones he'd snuck through the basement's window. They rested inside the straw like precious cargo.

In the morning, while all the girls were asleep, he'd been able to come in through the basement window, and sneak a few detonator mines into hiding places near the entrances and exits of the building just in case things went sour. Their blasts were powerful but compact; still, he'd rather not use them unless he absolutely had too. Explosives could be useful, but one mistake would get you killed, not to mention the potential for collateral damage.

Murphy took two of the pineapple grenades and strapped them to his belt; the rest he left in the crate. He carried a tommy gun, black iron and brown wood, strapped around his back. On his hip, he wore his Magnum in a holster.

He walked toward the steps of the basement and checked his watch. 1:59 P.M. He heard a feint knock from the bordello's front door, and the tap of footsteps above him. A minute early, but that would be okay; the girls had woken up an hour ago. Murphy heard muffled voices. He gripped his gun and leaned against the wall at the bottom of the steps, looking up toward the door. And waited for Rudi's signal.

* * * * *

"Greetings, *fräulein*," Rudi said. "I have an appointment here with Sammy Gambino and a Mr. Thomas Hughes. May I come inside?"

"Come in, come in," the woman at the door beckoned him. She wore a ruby red corset over fishnet stockings and heels; her left leg and a garter belt came out from a silk robe she wore open over her body. She blew smoke from her cigarette out of the side of her mouth and moved aside so he could enter. To Rudi, she was quite gorgeous, dark skin with lips painted crimson, round cheeks and a small mouth, her tight curls pulled into braids. From the memory of Dee's photo, he could see she wasn't Murphy's sister.

She pointed her long, slender black cigarette holder down the hallway and told him, "They're waiting for you in the dining room."

Rudi nodded toward the woman, took off his hat and walked inside. He walked down a long, narrow corridor, past the basement's doorway, until it eventually opened up into a dining room to his left opposite a modest parlor. Sammy Gambino and Thomas Hughes were sitting at the dining room table, sipping coffee. Sammy looked bored, but Hughes was nervous and sweating, his shirt and vest damp around the armpits. Four other men were seated, two with guns slung around the back of their chairs.

"Thomas," Rudi said, "it is good to finally meet you."

"Likewise, Mr. Rudiger," Hughes replied.

"Have a seat," Sammy told him.

Rudi sat down in the only empty chair. He placed his hands on the table. "You brought what was promised, *ja*?" he asked Hughes expectantly.

"Indeed," Hughes replied. "It's in this briefcase, have a look." He slid the briefcase over, and it opened with a snap and a click.

Rudi looked inside. They certainly looked like blueprints, schematics for some kind of aero-plane, one he'd never seen before.

"Very well," Rudi told him. "But I represent another interested party. I need to meet the proprietor of this fine establishment, and thank her in person for all of her hospitality."

"She ain't here," Sammy said, his eyebrow cocked with suspicion. "What's she to you, anyway, bub? Been gettin' a lot of questions about her lately."

"I am a foreign intelligence agent for the Third Reich, and it would be good for us to have friendly accommodations in New York," Rudi explained. "But I need to meet the woman in charge to make such an assessment. I'm sure you understand? Otherwise, I'm not permitted to take these documents, nor grant you the sum we agreed upon, Mr. Hughes."

"You'll want these," Hughes said, a note of desperation in his voice. "Take the designs now, or you won't see anything like them again until they're in the sky over Berlin."

"*Nein*," Rudi dismissed Hughes with a curt slash of his hand. "Where is Diane Lee? My superiors have taken an interest in her. She could be of use to us."

Sammy exchanged a glance with Hughes, and looked back at Rudi, his eyes narrowed. "She ain't here. And I don't care what the Reich wants or does not want. You cough up that dough, or I'll plug you and take it off your corpse!"

Rudi pounded on the table and stood up, stomping his foot loud enough for Murphy to hear. *"Nein!"* he pulled his Luger from the holster at his hip and fired a round into the head of Gambino's man who was sitting next to him. Rudi made a move toward the briefcase, but Gambino aimed a pulse gun he'd pulled from his coat straight at Rudi's face. A spiral shaped bolt of purple energy, a "tesla-beam" in the common parlance, flew over Rudi's head as he ducked beneath the table.

I'll be damned, Rudi thought, *an experimental weapon. Only one way to even the odds.* From underneath the table, Rudi fired more rounds with his Luger at all the kneecaps he could see. A hideous wail of agony told him that at least one of his shots had hit its mark. Rudi gripped the bottom of the table, and heaved it over in the direction of Sammy and Hughes, papers, coffee cups, table cloth and stirring spoons clanging and shattering on the floor. A half dozen bullets followed him out into the hallway, but none found him.

"Duck," Murphy told Rudi from near the Bordello's entrance. He fired a torrent from his tommy gun that ripped through the corridor, keeping Hughes, Gambino, and his men inside the dining room.

Screams erupted from the top of the steps, wailing shrieks from the girls and angry yells punctuated with savage curses from the few men who had arrived early. Clattering footsteps made their way down the fire escape at the rear of the building. Within moments, the upstairs was quiet. The woman who'd let Rudi in scrambled through the front door. Eli turned sideways then stepped inside before the door shut again behind him. He had his pistol drawn and pointed in front of him.

"Hughes!" Eli called down the corridor. "Come out with the case, both hands holding onto it. Surrender."

There was no response. Silence filled the hallway's gun-smoke haze. The three men crept forward quietly, Murphy leading them past the yellowed wall-paper and nude portraits that had not changed since he was a boy, except for one frame whose glass had cracked and another that was gone completely, leaving behind a gold halo surrounding a pale empty space.

As Murphy's eyes fell upon the halo, it transformed into a black void surrounded by an orange ring of flame, burst apart by the purple spiral of a tesla-beam. It flew past Murphy's face and into the wall of the corridor behind them, leaving another sizzling hole.

"You're outgunned, boys!" Gambino called out from the dining room. As if to punctuate this sentiment, Gambino's two remaining men ran across the corridor into the parlor and fired a few rounds from the corner until Murphy fired back and they ducked back into cover.

"I'm going to ring the bell in three," Murphy spoke calmly.

"I need Hughes alive," Eli hissed.

"Two," Murphy said.

"Ready," Rudi crouched on one knee with his Luger pointed down the hallway.

"One," Murphy hit a button on the detonator inside his pocket and a thundering *boom* of explosive, plaster, brick and mortar blasted above the rear entrance of the Bordello. Murphy rushed down the corridor with his Magnum held in front of him, firing into the parlor at the sound of hacking coughs that fought to breathe through the dust and debris from the explosion. Two shots howled through the smoke and dust; the room fell silent.

Eli and Rudi entered the dining room and found Hughes huddled beneath the table, an embarrassing puddle forming beneath the wet seat of his trousers. Gambino had been knocked unconscious by a fragment of the debris. The gun that fired the Tesla beam was a pistol of chrome and leather. It ended in a sharp point surrounded by a round metal dish. "Interesting design," Rudi said, picking up the gun.

Eli brought Hughes up to his feet. "Compose yourself, Hughes," Eli grunted. "You're still alive, at least for now. May God have mercy on you; I fear England will not."

"Hold on," Murphy spoke. "Did you hear somebody go up the fire escape?"

"I didn't hear anything," Rudi said.

"Nor I," Eli said, "but it's best we leave, regardless. Murphy, do you care to finish the job on Gambino? I certainly wouldn't blame you."

"As a matter of fact—"

Murphy's sentence was interrupted by three loud cracks from

behind them in the corridor. Eli's jacket tore open at the shoulder and blood poured from the tunnel between two wounds. Murphy and Rudi ducked into the parlor, but Eli lay defenseless in the hallway. Hughes crouched back under the dining room table.

"Murphy," Eli grunted, "I think I found your sister."

3

"Drop the gun. Slide it to me." Dee delivered her instructions clearly and precisely. Her voice lacked emotion, but communicated urgency. Eli obeyed and slid the pistol down the hallway. She stopped it with her foot then picked it up. Dee aimed both guns at Eli, who remained on the ground.

"We're all professionals," Dee called out. "Nobody else needs to get hurt. Murphy, take your friend out the window. The blueprints stay with me. Eli's my hostage until we make a deal. I see hide or hair of either of you before I get my money, you and the limey are good as dead. *Capiche*?"

Murphy had to stifle a chuckle. His older sister had more guts than most gangsters, and more brains. A loose cannon would've murdered Eli as soon as he got the chance, until only one man was left standing, but Dee knew better.

"*Capiche*," Murphy replied. "You can find my number on the tele-net. I'm opening the window now. Don't shoot."

Rudi nodded. They holstered their weapons. Rudi held onto the pulse gun. Hughes and the blueprints remained inside the dining room, as far out of reach as if they were on the other side of the world. Rudi sighed, and climbed onto the fire escape. Their footsteps clanged down the steps.

"I hope you're worth more alive than dead. What's your name?" Dee asked.

"Eli Jacobs," he told her. "I'm an Agent of the British Crown. Kill me, and you'll have all the force of Scotland Yard and the FBI fall upon you."

Dee laughed. "Ain't that how it always is? Get up."

Eli grunted, and sat up against the wall. He leaned against it, and pushed himself up, leaving a smear of blood behind. He'd been hurt worse, but knew he'd need to be stitched up soon. Already his skin was pale and he felt a chill.

"There's a bathroom opposite the door to the basement," Dee pointed to a door near the Bordello's front entrance. "Go inside. I'll patch you up."

Eli nodded and followed her into the bathroom. She tore his shirt at the shoulder seam and winced. "At least it's a flesh wound. Missed your collar bone and shoulder blade. Don't think I could manage that again if I tried." She poured from a brown bottle of hydrogen peroxide; the wound bubbled and foamed with a soft hiss. Next, she wrapped a bandage around the exit wound. Eli was lucky. His thick blood kept him from bleeding out. Already, his wound had slowed to a steady trickle.

"Your bedside manner is as good as your aim. You sure you can keep Gambino from killing me?" Eli asked.

"I'll give him a cut of whatever I get from your embassy. He'll understand." Dee brought a needle and thread from the mirror above the sink, lit a match, and burned the tip of the needle. "Lean back and think of England," she said as she dug the needle into his flesh, the black thread cinching his skin together. Eli winced.

"Haven't been stitched up since 1918," Eli grunted in pain.

"That how you lost the eye?" Dee asked.

"I didn't lose it. I left it behind," Eli said. "Artillery shrapnel. Could've been worse. I met some eunuchs in the field hospital."

"Turn around. I'll take care of the other side."

Eli looked at himself in the mirror. He glanced back at Dee and they locked eyes. "Do you miss your brother?"

"Sometimes," Dee admitted. "He's got no head for business. Everything's so personal for him. Complicates things."

"Seems like you two could learn a lot from each other," Eli said. "You're all business."

"Ain't that the truth," Dee sighed. "I've been in this game a long time, and stopped caring years ago. I seen some shit, Eli."

"Well, in spite of what's happened in the past, you've obviously done quite well for yourself. What's next?" he asked.

"We're going to call your embassy. Find out how much a spy, a traitor, and those blueprints are worth."

* * * * *

The phone rang. Murphy and Rudi looked up from their bourbon. "Answer it," Murphy instructed.

"Hello?" Rudi answered. "Speaking. *Ja. Ja.* Understood." He hung up the phone.

"You need to contact Dee. She's to bring everything to the embassy. They've already granted her immunity; they even have paperwork. All she has to do is hand over Eli, Hughes and the blueprints," Rudi explained.

"She won," Murphy whispered.

"Don't they always?" Rudi sighed.

Murphy picked up the phone. He held the earpiece to his ear and dialed the number. The drone of the dial tone hummed as he waited for someone to pick up. "I need to speak to Diane Lee. Tell her it's Murphy. Yeah, Dee."

Rudi took another drag off the roach. His bourbon was dry so he poured some water from the faucet.

"Let me hit that," Murphy said. He held out his hand as he waited. A startled cough erupted. "Dee?" he said in a breath of smoke. He took a sip of Rudi's water. "We need to pick you up. We're going to the embassy. Leave Gambino at the Bordello. I know he wants his cut, but he'll just have to trust you. Six o'clock. How's Eli doing?"

Rudi listened to Murphy's half of the conversation. His head swam. He'd not smoked hashish since visiting Istanbul before the war, but this American leaf felt like listening to jazz in the bayou, the taste of molasses, and the smell of honeysuckle. At least, that is how he imagined it in the moment.

"Rudi?" Murphy called, pulling him from his reverie.

"*Ja?*" Rudi asked. "What did she say?"

"We need to take the train to the Bordello. One of Eli's men will pick us up in a limousine. Can you believe that? The embassy will get Hughes, Eli got his man, I found my sister, and you'll go to

England. Everybody got what they were looking for," Murphy said with a sad nonchalance.

Rudi smiled. "Your sister owes you a cut of the take. Perhaps she'll even hire you."

"I won't work for Dee no more," Murphy said, "but I'll take her money. C'mon, we got to go."

Rudi shook his head. "I need some coffee."

"We'll get some at the platform. They just installed new server bots. The Service Union has blown some to hell, but when they work, they make damn fine coffee. And you don't have to tip them," Murphy said.

"Fuck Tesla and fuck Ford. Fuck Hitler, Chamberlain and Roosevelt," Rudi spoke in a rant.

"You're goddamned right about that. Now c'mon, we need to go." Murphy led him down into the subway. He looked around them and peered with his third eye, but could feel no one followed them underground. Murphy had learned to trust his intuition long ago.

Rudi pointed out a coffee stand. A pair of men stood behind the counter in white paper hats. "I thought they laid you off. Two espressos," Murphy ordered.

"We came to an understanding," one of the men explained. "We work during the day, the bots take the night shift. We stop blowing up the bots."

"Sounds like a gentleman's agreement," Rudi said.

They grabbed their drinks and headed onto to the train. Its hydraulic doors opened with a hiss of steam, and the magnetic force of the track held the car a few inches in the air. They sipped their espresso, and watched the world rush by in a blurred streak. Suddenly, they came out onto an elevated track. Afternoon sun shined through the windows of the train. Rudi welcomed it. It helped him be alert, focused. The coffee helped too.

Eventually, the train glided into Harlem. The doors opened and a mass of humanity shuffled out. Vendors on the platform offered barbecued ribs, cooked in huge smokers by some burly men who hailed from Alabama. No way a simple bot could ever replace those two. Their sauce was said to contain a certain kind of bayou magic, and whether or not the voodoo actually worked, Murphy knew many wives who made their husbands eat there regularly.

Rudi inhaled, taking in the scent of barbecue smoke, boiled peanuts and beer. in the summer-time , the platform had an atmosphere that was almost carnivalesque. In the winter, these same booths would sell coffee and whiskey, as metal drums warmed hands with a crackling blaze, and vagrants begged for coin beneath tattered blankets. Rudi could almost see them. It was the same at the platforms in Manhattan, only the workers wore suit and tie instead of a laborer's blue coveralls. He imagined the trains in Berlin, the scent of pretzels and sauerkraut, the sweet taste of strudel at Christmas. Rudi imagined he might never see his fatherland again in this lifetime.

"Stay sharp, Rudi," Murphy told him. "Keep your hand on that Luger. These are desperate times."

They walked side by side down the streets of Harlem into the red light district. The sun had crept low in the sky, and as the heat fell to a simmer, young men and women walked around in ragged posses. One or two might cast an eye on Eli, but Murphy warned them off with a grim look.

"I recognize this neighborhood," Rudi said eventually. "We are almost here."

"Are you ready?" Murphy asked him.

"As I'll ever be," Rudi replied.

"Just follow my lead. Keep an eye out for Gambino's men, just in case," Murphy said, and then knocked on the Bordello's tall door.

Dee answered. Murphy's eyes widened in surprise. He had never seen her dress so well. She wore a navy blue skirt down to her knees, cut with a very modest slit. Her legs were bare underneath, a concession to the heat, but she also wore a smart navy blue jacket with gold buttons. Rudi was reminded of the uniforms of American civil war soldiers, but no general ever wore navy and gold so well. Her feet were bare too, but a pair of unlaced black loafers was tucked beneath a coat rack nearby.

"Ain't never seen a lady lookin' so classy? I don't doubt it. Come in, and mind your jaw lest you trip over it. How are you, Rudi?" Dee welcomed the pair inside.

Eli was sitting at the kitchen table, wearing a sleeveless white undershirt, a bulky white bandage covering his shoulder. A glass cup in front of him beaded water down its surface. Ice cubes and bubbles tinkled as he took a sip of the tonic. A green bottle of gin rested beside him, half empty. Instead of his glass eye, he wore an eye-patch. "I'm off duty for another half hour. You boys are early. Sit down and share a drink with us."

Murphy remained silent, but nodded and grabbed a seat. He took off his hat and jacket, and laid his shoulder holster down on the table. He poured himself and Rudi a drink with just a splash of gin for each of them. With his sister was around, he meant to stay alert.

"Do you know who invented the gin and tonic?" Eli asked. "The British, of course! My grandparents used it in India as a way to disguise the taste of quinine, a preventative medicine for malaria. Otherwise, they'd risk yellow fever. These days, it's the taste and gin we enjoy, but back then, it was a matter of life and death."

"Thank you, professor," Murphy spoke in a slow drawl.

Dee smiled. "It's good to hear your voice again, Murphy. Rudi, Eli, could you excuse us?"

The two men got to their feet and sauntered into the parlor. Dee sat in front of Murphy and crunched some ice from her drink. Delicately, she placed one of her hands over Murphy's. When he didn't flinch or look away, she stared into his eyes. Murphy looked back, and felt himself falling deep inside them, the whites almost a pale yellow surrounded by skin the color of black coffee, of fertile soil, of burnt hickory. Against her skin, he was almost pale, but he could see himself in her pupils and the way she cocked her head. The strength of her hands was almost masculine, but the rest of her had a queen's majesty. He couldn't help but look away, and blink a tear from his eye.

"I never meant for you to find me like that. Clumsy, I know. I'm glad you were able to stay out of trouble," she said.

"I'm sorry I blamed you. I know you were just doing your job. But when I saw my sergeant's shit-eating grin, I couldn't help myself. I saw in him the father I never knew, and I saw our mother in you," he explained.

"That's over now. I mean to retire," Dee told him.

"What do you mean?" he asked.

"I'm selling the Bordello. Moving out of the Gambinos' territory altogether. I intend to invest some of my money into heroin distribution. I'll be a silent partner to some Triads in Chinatown. The rest will be in a nest-egg. And since Mama gave me the deed, I can live off the interest. Completely legitimate," she softly explained. Dee still hadn't taken her hand off of his.

Murphy looked back up at her. "Still living off the misery of others? I guess I can't blame you. Misery is all we've ever known."

"No, not the only thing," Dee whispered. "I've grown quite fond of your partner." She smiled. "Perhaps what I need is an older man. Or some other kind. Why don't you work for me? I can offer you a hefty retainer. You could be my bodyguard. Come to meetings with me. Flex some muscle from time to time. Otherwise, do what you will. You can be a brother to me. Or not. Perhaps someday you'll remember how to."

"I was always your brother, Dee," Murphy whispered. "That's why I came looking for you. I thought you were in trouble. But it was really us who were in trouble the whole god-damned time. You straightened this mess out."

"Little ol' me?" she asked with a laugh.

Murphy sighed. His nose was stuffed up, so he breathed in deeply and pinched the bridge of his nose. "Let's be a family again. But not partners. I need to find my own path."

"Fair enough," Dee told him. "But I won't let you be too proud to ask for help. No brother of mine is going to live off cat-food and tap-water."

"Agreed," Murphy said. "And whether or not we're in business together, you still owe me for today. With the money you've got coming, I could open up a real office, maybe even hire a secretary. Find some decent clientele."

"One step at a time, little brother," Dee replied. They finally unclasped each other's hands, clinked their glasses together, and drank the rest of their tonics. An impatient burst from a car horn broke the silence.

"Come on then," Eli spoke, putting his jacket around his shirt, still un-tucked and un-buttoned.

"To yellow fever!" Rudi said, and knocked back the rest of his drink.

The four of them walked down the steps of the Bordello and stepped into a white limousine with black tinted windows. Hughes was placed in the front seat where he could be kept under the chauffeur's supervision. A valet in a crisp black and white uniform held the door open for the rest of the passengers. Murphy and Dee entered first and took the seat facing forward. Rudi and Eli sat opposite them.

Eli grinned and hoped for a holiday once this sordid business was finally taken care of. Rudi imagined diving from the white cliffs of Dover, and considered how he would bring the rest of his family out of Germany before the storm broke. A quiet peace settled over them.

Dee rested her head on Murphy's shoulder; he wrapped his arm around her in a protective embrace. She had always taken care of him, until he no longer let her. It would be good for the two of them to begin taking care of each other.

Author's Note: *Since writing this story, the author has learned that malaria and yellow fever are two distinct mosquito-borne illnesses. The information regarding the origin of the gin and tonic, quinine, and the prevention of malaria remain true.*

Please excuse the remnants of the author's ignorance that remain in this story. He has an attachment to the story's original title.

Thanks for reading.

The Adventures of Baxter and Roebuck

Episode I: Time to Remember what I forgot

Baxter smelled the smokestacks before he was ever able to see them. The scent reminded him of home, a smothering sweetness that hung thick in the air. He gripped his throttle with a gloved hand and gunned it, his engine answering with an angry growl and a loud pop. His goggles were smeared with bug guts, but through the goo and antenna, he saw the road become smooth and the cacti begin to blur. The needle on his speedometer crossed one hundred, but Baxter failed to notice. He rode an ancient black Harley, as fast and loud as a tornado.

Beside him, ROEBUCK kept pace. His cycle seemed to hum, calm in comparison to Baxter's. The bot's steel exterior was coated in a thin layer of road-dust, but his bright red visual scanner shined like a ruby through the grime as it gathered data about the landscape. "Approaching. Our destination is three point seven miles away," ROEBUCK announced in an electronic monotone. His bike was a sleek Kawasaki, as sharp as a katana, twice as deadly.

The bot defied any kind of logic. Robots, as a species, were still very rudimentary, at least for the most part. They were good for making things and even some conveniences, like those cars that knew how to drive themselves. ROEBUCK exceeded these and all other expectations of what a machine could be. Baxter had asked him to explain this once. ROEBUCK told him he came from the future. Baxter didn't know whether to believe him or not. He had a deadpan sense of humor. These were a time of legends, so ROEBUCK seemed to speak and walk like something from a movie. And since so much technology from before the Great Fall was still misunderstood, most people accepted him as a curious novelty.

ROEBUCK rode through the twilight like a silver bullet. Ahead of him, the sun bled red and heavy in the sky, lighting the purple clouds with a crimson glow. The moon was a feint silver sickle. As if weaving the clouds from white smoke, a row of smokestacks rose on the horizon. Along the outskirts, among canvas tents and tin shanties, the cloying scent of the distillery covered everything.

"My olfactory sensors are overwhelmed," ROEBUCK said as they slowed their cycles to a gentle pace. The inhabitants of the slums swarmed around them as they neared the bustling town's twilight market.

"You'll get used to it," Baxter told him, as he swung his leg over his seat and began to walk his cycle. "Let's get off these for a sec. I want to poke around a little."

"As you wish," ROEBUCK said and did the same. A rattling vibration passed through the bot and the dust of the road shook off him. Underneath the sand, his steel body gleamed smooth, welded seams and tiny rivets between the metal plates. He wore a black suit with a white collared shirt and a thin black tie that ended in a flat rectangular tip. It was an impeccable outfit, as always.

Baxter's gear was more of a mismatch of items, picked up here and there over many seasons on the road. His helmet was black and white, and had a circle with an eight stenciled onto it to resemble a billiard ball. He wore a brown leather jacket patched and stitched together with a mix of ragged materials. On his hip, he carried a Magnum revolver, jewel encrusted, with an ivory handle and shining chrome barrel. It was his one indulgence, which he owned proudly and knew well how to wield. His right hand never strayed far from it.

One of the street vendors, a short brown man with a thick mass of gray curls nodded in his direction. "Baxter! It's good to see you. It's been a while. We thought maybe you bought it." He stood behind a white counter next to a steaming grill full of ostrich burgers and potato fries. Baxter's throat was parched, and he swallowed when he saw the rows of beer lined up in a glass cooler.

"Couple of cold ones, Mac," Baxter ordered as he stretched his goggles onto his helmet, and pulled his bandana down around his neck. A thin line of dirt remained in the space between them. Baxter wiped away the grit with the back of his hand. "Much obliged. Been on the road a while. Me and ROEBUCK had business back east. One thing led to another. Spent a couple of years criss-crossing Texas and Mexico with a band of *banditos*. Beside the bot, I ain't got much to show for it. Thought I'd see what's shaking back home."

"Hmm," Mac considered this for a moment. "Ain't too much that's changed. The Alexander's still run the distillery; have half the town on their payroll. The rest of us toil to feed, clothe, and house the families who work for them. Sandstorms ain't been too bad as of late. Got a new radar dish installed on Mount Whitepeak, lets us know when the winds are picking up."

"Radar," ROEBUCK remarked. "How primitive."

"Watch your tin mouth, before I decide to weld it shut," Baxter growled as he gave his partner a sidelong glance. "Show some manners. This here's an old friend."

ROEBUCK warbled a series of beeps that had the tone of rotten obscenities.

"Know anybody who's hiring?" Baxter asked.

"Well, not nobody that needs a hired gun. Things are pretty peaceful as of late. Alexander's police see to that," Mac explained.

"Poh-lice," Baxter pronounced the word like a curse and spat into the sand. He slammed his second empty bottle of beer on the counter. "One more beer and a burger and fries to go. Thanks, Mac." He threw down a handful of nine millimeter bullets, universal currency in a world where the local scrip could be anything from lizard pelts to coupons from the company store.

Baxter found an empty spot on the curb and popped the cap off his beer bottle. He opened the paper bag Mac had given him and breathed in the familiar aroma of ostrich burgers and greasy french-fries cooked in peanut oil. The salty fries made him thirst and he swigged his beer, a three percent brew that had just enough alcohol to keep one safe from the flux but still sharp enough to aim a gun barrel. Baxter let out a loud belch as he finished his meal, crumbled his bag and threw his litter on top of a wire rim trash can already overflowing with rubbish.

"It's getting late. I need to find us some accommodations," Baxter said.

"An oil bath would certainly be welcome," ROEBUCK replied. "Perhaps a washing machine in working order."

"Well, it won't be nothing fancy, but I got a friend, owes me a few favors. Think he'll let us crash," Baxter told him as they began walking their cycles again. The sun had finally set, so the lamps lit one by one, burning blue and yellow, sharp with the tang of ethanol.

* * * * *

"You've got a hell of a lot of nerve coming here."

"Hey, Julie," Baxter greeted her. "Rick here?"

"Who is it?" a voice called from inside the trailer. A feint whiff of stale cigarettes wafted out, giving the odor of the distillery a musty coat.

"It's our old fucking friend, Baxter," she called behind her. "And the Tin Man. You deal with them. I'm outta here."

Baxter stepped aside as she left, muttering a curse under her breath. He turned and walked inside, bringing ROEBUCK with him.

Rick leaned heavily on a black iron cane as he studied Baxter. His green eyes were creased beneath a freckled brow, slicked red hair combed back. "Good to see you again," he said, shaking Baxter's hand. "Who's your bot? Looks fancy."

"Rick, let me introduce you to my partner, ROEBUCK," Baxter said.

"Greetings," ROEBUCK looked around. "How cozy."

"Any pal of Baxter's a pal of mine." Rick smiled. "Well sit down. I'll get you a beer, Baxter."

"Much obliged," Baxter replied, settling into a chair. "I guess Julie's still sore."

"Ah, don't mind her," Rick said, leaning into the open fridge. "She still blames you for the car. And the leg."

"Can't say's I blame her," Baxter said. "I *was* driving that night."

"Yeah, but the job was my idea," Rick said, handing Baxter the beer once he'd popped off its cap. He gripped his cane as he settled down into an easy chair.

"Well, I've always been an enabler," Baxter grunted. "Shit man, I guess I got to say, we was wondering if you could help us out. Think I can crash on your couch a few nights? ROEBUCK just needs a place to power down. I need time to hustle up some work."

Rick whistled. "Now you know I'd catch hell for that."

"Ain't got no other choice," Baxter pleaded. "But seeing here as our last score let you put a down payment on this beauty, I figure this trailer's half mine anyway."

"At least you get to keep earning," Rick said tapping his knee with his knuckles. "You can stay tonight. I got a contact, might get you some delivery work. It'll be dangerous."

"That's alright with me and ROEBUCK. Danger is lucrative," Baxter told him, eyes gleaming gold.

Rick chuckled. "Guess that's true."

"Your record player still working?" Baxter asked.

"Hell yeah," Rick said as he flipped a switch on the cabinet behind him. The trill of surf music from before the Great Fall came pouring out the speakers. "Got this from a salt caravan."

"'Misirlou' by Dick Dale, 1962," ROEBUCK said.

"Don't mind him," Baxter said. "Electric encyclopedia. But that comes in handy sometimes."

* * * * *

The crooked finger of dawn parted the curtains of the trailer's window and poked red in Baxter's eyes. He sat up on his bed, stretched and yawned. From the kitchen, the coffee pot rumbled and hissed.

A metal spatula scraped a cast-iron frying pan cooking on the stove. Rick flipped the pan a couple of times and some scrambled eggs whipped around. Pork was too expensive for Baxter to hope for bacon, but the coffee and eggs were enough. It smelled like Rick was toasting some home-made bread to go along with it.

Baxter stood up and noticed the thin band of black plastic that housed ROEBUCK's optical sensors begin to glow red. "Good morning, Baxter. I'm going to go outside and recharge." Baxter nodded. The bot's surface was covered in tiny but extremely sensitive solar panels. He only needed a quarter of an hour in direct sunlight, at most a few hours on cloudy and dreary days, to completely recharge.

With gasoline worth more than its weight in gold, people had learned to use other kinds of energy in the decades since the Great Fall. Those dark times had been lived by Baxter's grandparents, but at least they and a few of everyone else's ancestors had been among the precious, lucky few to survive the plagues and wars of the twenty-first century. Whatever his origins, ROEBUCK was well adapted to this new world.

He let the door of the trailer shut behind him while Baxter sat down for breakfast.

"Morning," Rick grunted as he scraped eggs onto Baxter's plate, his cigarette flaking ashes close to their meal. Rick walked back to the stove, turned it off, ground out his cigarette in an ashtray resting on the window sill, and sat down at the kitchen table with two mugs of coffee.

The men ate for a few moments of hungry silence. With their bellies full and their brains lubricated with caffeine, Rick spoke. "You can't stay here. I wish it were different, but Julie ain't come back last night, and she's the only one of us still draws a paycheck. " He lit a fresh cigarette and offered one to Baxter.

"I understand," Baxter growled, lighting up. "Think you can help me find some work?" The cigarettes' haze filled the cramped trailer.

"Go to the foreman at this address," Rick slid a piece of paper with an address in the manufacturing district. "He's got a caravan, and he's shipping six thousand gallons of ethanol to Rock Springs, a mining town 'bout a hundred miles to the northwest. We got raiders, been causing him problems. Man's already hired an escort, but I'll wager he'll pay for a couple extra guns."

"How you know about this?" Baxter asked. He stood up from the table, cracked the kitchen window, and blew his smoke outside.

"I do favors for him sometimes," Rick explained. "I introduced him to my buddy Lester. They've helped him with a few escorts. Lester's men eat better than the raiders in these parts, and at least he's sane."

Baxter nodded. "Much obliged for the room and board. And the smoke," he said, stubbing out his cigarette. "Give my regards to Julie."

"It was good to see you," Rick said as Baxter opened the door. "Don't come back."

* * * * *

Baxter and ROEBUCK pulled up to the address Rick gave them. The rumble of their engines faded for a few moments until they killed their ignitions. A sweet scent of burned ethanol clung to the air as Baxter removed his bandana and goggles from his face.

"A modest operation," ROEBUCK observed.

A uniformed man walked out of a small guard shack. "You got business here?" he asked. His moustache and buzz-cut were white peppered with steel grey, but the gun on his hip had not aged.

"We heard your boss is looking for muscle. His caravan left yet?" Baxter asked.

"No, but it's about to," the guard replied. "Speak to Lester. He's leading 'em. Take your cycles with you. The big boss will pay you when you get back. If you get back."

Baxter didn't like the grin in the old man's voice, but he ignored the comment and approached the caravan, idling in an otherwise empty lot nearby. Surrounding an ancient 16-wheeled freighter, were a collective of motorcycles, pick-up trucks, and some kind of humvee with a machine gun mounted on its canopy. Like almost every vehicle still in operation, they ran on whatever kind of biofuel was available. Corn from the plains was trucked to the desert, because that's where the biggest refineries and distilleries still operated. Farmland was too valuable to waste on space for factories and distilleries, so harvests were shipped to the desert to be made into fuel.

"You Lester?" Baxter asked a grizzled mercenary dressed in leather and chains. He had spikes on the knuckles of his gloves, and his brown beard was grizzled and half-gray. A veteran. *Must be a hell of a fighter to have lived so long,* Baxter reflected. ROEBUCK stood silently beside them.

Lester grunted, "Mmhmm." He glanced up and down at Baxter and

ROEBUCK. He spotted Baxter's ivory-handled pistol and let out a low whistle. "You know how to use that?" he pointed at the gun.

"'Course I do," Baxter spat into the dust beside him.

"And the bot?" Lester asked.

"I can speak for myself, thank you," ROEBUCK replied. "My weapons are concealed but formidable."

Lester snorted. "You'll do. Raiders have been hell lately, but Rock Springs is sending out some of their militia to meet us halfway. They're desperate for the ethanol, so they need us to get through."

"Simple enough," Baxter said.

He got onto his cycle, and revved his engine, pulled goggles over his eyes and lifted his bandana over his nose and mouth. Lester nodded, and got into the passenger seat of a gun-mounted pick-up truck. The pick-up honked its horn a couple times, and the 16-wheeler responded with a loud blast from its horn. Lester's caravan rolled out, Baxter and ROEBUCK scouting a half-mile ahead with the other motorcycles to act as scouts for the rest of the vehicles.

In an hour's time, a cloud of dust followed them, the distant horizon wide and flat. The border between desert and sky blurred in the heat.

* * * * *

The road to Rock Springs was long and cruel. Scrubs and bushes grew on the side of the road, dry and scraggly. Tumbleweed drifted past, blowing in the desert wind. Every once in a while, Baxter could see a few birds circle in the sky, or an armadillo run across the road. He glanced at ROEBUCK. Riding on his right hand. As always.

ROEBUCK's optic sensors could see for miles. Some life forms glowed bright from the heat of their bodies. Others were as cool as the rocks. His senses were more powerful than a human's. And he possessed some senses humans didn't, like the ability to sense the entire electro-magnetic spectrum.

On the horizon, he sensed something different. Metal. Cold as the night.

"Slow down," he told Baxter. "There's an IED up ahead."

"Hell," Baxter said. "Get ready."

Baxter tried to signal Lester to warn his bikers about the trap they were about to run into, but it was too late. A few dozen yards ahead of them, one of the motorcycles blew up in a streak of fire and rubber. The rider's body fell back onto the road, a column of smoke rising into the air from the remnants.

The caravan screeched to a halt. The riders peered into the distance through binoculars and telescopes smeared with sweat and dust, but couldn't see anything except sand and sky. Seconds stretched into minutes. Eventually, Lester motioned the caravan to continue, slowly, so that ROEBUCK could warn them of any more bombs.

A howling streak came hurtling across the landscape and struck one of the pick-up trucks with a rocket-propelled grenade. The caravan scattered like a herd of frightened animals. Baxter gunned his cycle, hoping his luck would hold out against remaining IED's. Crouched behind a sand dune, he found a squad of men camouflaged behind a few sandbags. They were loading a mortar, but reached for their guns as soon as they saw Baxter. He fired his pistol six times, and the only shots the mortar team got off were wild and aimless, clutching their triggers as they died in the sand. Baxter spun his bike around and sped away back toward the rest of the caravan.

And then the hum of motorcycles surrounded them like a swarm of angry bees. Dozens of bikes, raider mods, full of spikes and machine guns sped around the caravan's ragged huddle. The raiders were insane. They gunned their bikes full throttle, firing bullets past each other, nearly colliding with the random chaos of an electron cloud. A cloud of dust grew in their wake.

Baxter and ROEBUCK split from the rest of the caravan's escort. Baxter wheeled left, skidded to a stop, and fired from a spare nine millimeter into a cluster of raiders who'd bunched together. Three of the raiders fell, but one returned fire, the bullet bouncing off Baxter's rear fender. *A little too close for comfort*, he thought. He gunned his throttle and searched for other targets.

ROEBUCK's weapon was a hand-cannon. His right hand and wrist transformed into a Gatling-style gun that fired a torrent of bullets at the scattered raiders, but since he had to fire wide to avoid hitting other members of the caravan, he only managed to puncture a tire.

But he convinced the raiders to flee. Unable to cripple the rig, they left to hunt easier prey.

* * * * *

"Could've used you back there," Lester told the captain. "We're so close to Rock Springs, you might as well throw down a welcome mat."

"This is the rendezvous we agreed on," the captain replied. "If you didn't like it, you should've said something last week." He was wearing a military uniform made from scavenged mixed-up gear. A patch on the captain's chest read "Boone", but it wasn't clear that that was his actual name.

"That you? Boone?" Baxter asked.

"Jim Boone, Rock Springs Special Defense. Good to meet ya," Boone shook hands with Baxter. Then he caught sight of ROEBUCK. "Damn, son. I ain't never seen a bot this advanced."

"This is my partner, ROEBUCK," Baxter introduced him.

ROEBUCK nodded in Boone's direction and a flicker of red light ran across his optic sensor. "Good to make your acquaintance, Captain Boone. Are we far from Rock Springs?"

"Nah, not too far," Boone replied. "Just a hop, skip, and about twenty clicks away. Speaking of which, we're not gonna get any closer sitting here jawin' away. You ready to move out, Lester?"

"You're damned straight," Lester told him. He placed an index finger and a thumb in his mouth and blew until his cheeks puffed out. A powerful whistle ripped through the air. A chorus of ignitions and the hum of engines answered him. The caravan growled.

"How clever," ROEBUCK murmured. He turned to Baxter. "Can you do that?"

"No," Baxter said, "but I got a few tricks of my own. 'Sides, ain't much louder than a .45."

The caravan rumbled through the desert, which became rockier as they approached Rock Springs. The shadows grew long. Baxter took in the landscape around him, and appreciated the weirdness of it all;

arches of rock and boulders strangely balanced in surreal formations. It was a deceptive kind of fragility that was much more stubborn than it looked. Baxter imagined some kind of catastrophic force that could cause it all to come tumbling down like so many dominos.

After another few minutes on the road, Rock Springs emerged on the distant horizon as a ribbon of green and blue. Oases in this part of the desert were rare and valuable, like emeralds and sapphires scattered in the dust. Livestock and a few rows of crops were visible in the far distance. Wooden fences kept ostriches penned in, and a few members of the small herd looked up curiously as the caravan approached.

A grizzled old man in blue coveralls came out to meet Lester, Boone and the vanguard of the caravan. He had spots of grease on his clothes and a red bandana tucked into one of his pockets. "Bring her around to the tanks! We've got the pumps ready to go. Good job, boys."

A few members of the caravan began moving thick hoses and other equipment from the fuel truck, connecting nozzles and pipes to the tanks. A thirsty glugging came up from the pumps as the ethanol poured into tanks beneath the ground. Rock Springs had had trouble with the raiders countless times, so the subterranean tanks became a kind of insurance policy to make sure they always had enough fuel to power their machines.

"Alright," Lester announced, "we ain't got time to make it back tonight, but y'all have earned some R 'n' R. We'll meet here at sunrise. Anybody doesn't make it can fend for themselves."

"What are your plans?" ROEBUCK asked his companion.

"This here stream rambles on for a few miles," Baxter explained. "I'm gonna find me a place, wash off the grime of the road. Relax a bit. You're welcome to come with."

"It would be useful to analyze some local mineral samples," ROEBUCK replied. "Investigate the flora and fauna a bit."

"Whatever glides your gears, ROEBUCK."

* * * * *

The creek was cool and clear. The stones under the water were smooth and burnt red, a few covered in furry green algae. Baxter scooped some in his hands and brought it to his face, letting it trickle back down into the stream. It only reached his stomach even in the deepest parts, but he didn't mind. He crouched down and let the water cloak him, its gentle current unable to upset his balance.

Baxter relaxed completely as if cradled by gently rocking arms. The pebbles and plants beneath him waved to the rhythm of the water. All the heat and dust he'd gathered washed away. Even his heart beat in sync with the current. He felt oneness, a rare unity with the universe. He stared at his reflection, and found a rippling mirror. If only he could bottle up this sense of calm and bring it with him wherever he went; it could be a shield against the chaos of his existence. Instead, he opened every pore and dimension of his consciousness and let the waters wrap around every part of him.

ROEBUCK clicked and whirred as he wandered around the stream bed. He'd washed his clothes in the stream with a bar of lye he kept with him, and now they were steaming dry on a rock. He was focused on the minerals beneath him. In his analysis, ROEBUCK had lost himself too.

There were so many questions he could not answer. *Where had he come from? Who was his maker?* These could only confound him. But here he could grip certainty as a climber fingers hand-holds. The rust red of iron oxides. The golden yellow of limonite. Clay's damp sturdiness.

He pitied Baxter and other humans for the limits of their sensory instruments. ROEBUCK could see light that was infrared and ultraviolet, and magnify every particle thousands of times over. He could feel the light and heat of the sun and know exactly how far it had travelled. Yet he couldn't remember past the time Baxter had woken him in the laboratory deep beneath the sands of Los Alamos.

Somebody stole those memories from him, erased them. ROEBUCK could feel their absence, tingling like a phantom limb inside his consciousness. Every time he reached out to grasp them, the probing tendrils of his memory slipped past like fingers through ash. In the time he'd spent with Baxter, he'd formed new memories, and these he guarded well. He'd rather be destroyed than let them be forgotten.

"You alright, hombre? Been staring at that speck of dirt for the last five minutes," Baxter said as the water dripped off him.

ROEBUCK turned his head in Baxter's direction. "Conducting a deep spectral analysis. But it's over now. I'm ready to continue."

Baxter was rejuvenated. The heat of the afternoon sun felt good on his flesh as he and ROEBUCK dressed. They inspected their bikes for damage during the battle against the raiders but couldn't find much. A few holes made by buckshot, but nothing that would compromise "structural integrity" in ROEBUCK's words.

They mounted their bikes and made their way back into Rock Springs. Baxter found them a room to rent in the same motel as the rest of the caravan's members. Its flickering neon sign would make it easy to find when they made their way back in the middle of the night.

"I'm going to get some dinner and maybe a drink or two. How about you?" Baxter asked.

"We're in unfamiliar territory," ROEBUCK reminded him. "Best stick together."

* * * * *

The Rock-Steady Tavern was calm most evenings. A crowd of regulars sat at the bar, old timers sharing laughs with a busty middle-aged bartender, a towel on her shoulder and a pencil tucked behind her ear. Most of them didn't turn to look when they heard the front door open, but Baxter noticed the lady behind the bar make a slight double-take at the sight of ROEBUCK.

"Sit anywhere you like, fellas. Susie'll be right with you," she called out to them.

"Much obliged, ma'am," Baxter hollered back. He and ROEBUCK sat in one of the booths along the wall. The tavern was humble but comfortable. Dim lights reflected a sheen on the smooth wooden tables. A pre-war juke box even played country songs from across the room.

"Johnny Cash," ROEBUCK said. "Folsom Prison Blues."

"I'll take your word for it," Baxter grunted. "Seems pretty quiet, but just keep an eye out. Ain't in the mood for surprises."

ROEBUCK's optic sensors flared a brief acknowledgement. He turned his head slightly, and looked in the direction of approaching footsteps. Baxter followed his gaze.

"Good evening, boys," their server greeted them. She was a young blonde woman, short, slim; maybe even a teenager. Her voice had the rough edge of a smoker. "What can I get y'all?"

"I'll have a beer. What do you like to eat here?" Baxter asked.

"You like eggs?" the girl wanted to know.

"Unless they're raw," Baxter said.

"Get the ostrich omelet. You'll like it. He need anything?" she cocked her head in ROEBUCK's direction.

"No ma'am," ROEBUCK said.

"Be right back with your drink," she told them, and left to walk behind the bar.

In half a minute, she placed a cold bottle of beer on the table. Baxter took a sip, and leaned back against his bench. He hadn't felt this content and relaxed for a long time. "What you thinking about, partner?"

ROEBUCK looked up. "I was distracted by the wood grain on this table. I analyzed its age and density, and am scanning my database to determine the species. The stain makes it an uncertainty, but I believe it to be oak."

"Oak," Baxter replied. "That's a strong wood. My favorite is cedar, because of the smell. You reckon—"

The front door opened with a loud slam. A tear-streaked, gray-haired woman rushed inside and peered frightfully out the window. Baxter noticed the bartender reach under the bar. "Cover me, ROEBUCK."

He stood up from the table. His right hand gripped his revolver. The woman ducked beneath the window. The doors burst open again.

"Where is she?" a black-clad security soldier bellowed. He held a shotgun, but Baxter already had his revolver pointed in the man's face.

"This ain't your jurisdiction," Baxter told him. "It's mine. Leave the lady alone. Turn around and go. Tell your boss you couldn't find her."

"Why should I?" the soldier asked. He pointed his shotgun at Baxter.

ROEBUCK approached, his hand-cannon armed and ready to fire. "If you kill him, I'll kill you."

The soldier's eyes widened. He backed out of the bar and let the door close behind him.

"We'd better get out of here," Baxter told the gray-haired lady. Her clothes were dirty and frayed. She wore an old lab coat that used to be white. "You want to come with us?"

The woman nodded.

Baxter called behind the bar. "Gonna need that omelet to go!"

* * * * *

Baxter put the take-out into a case on his bike. He climbed on, flipped the ignition and gunned the engine. The motorcycle responded with an enthusiastic roar. "Get on back," he told the woman. She obeyed.

ROEBUCK got on his bike too. "We need to leave soon. Our friend's on his way back, and it looks like he brought company," the bot warned.

A security vehicle was creeping up the street in front of the tavern. Baxter and ROEBUCK rolled quietly down a nearby alley, but the cops saw them anyway. Their car's spotlight flooded the narrow space and its siren screamed in alarm. Red and blue lights spun and the alley lit up like a disco. The motorcycles sped away in a peel of burning rubber. "Hang on!" Baxter yelled to the woman behind him. She clutched tight.

The alley let out onto Slate Street, a four lane road with stoplights almost every block. Traffic was light this late at night. Baxter led the way. He weaved through cars and sped past intersections, ignoring red lights and honking horns. ROEBUCK kept up with him, but so did the security car.

Its heavy frame and powerful engine hurtled the vehicle through every obstacle in its way. Cars that couldn't move in time were brushed aside by a heavy metal bumper. The sound of broken glass and smacking metal created a cacophony with the screeching tires and wailing sirens. In the driver's seat, the cop who'd entered the bar floored the accelerator. From the passenger side and the back seat, two cops leaned out their windows and fired pistols at the motorcycles.

ROEBUCK felt the ping of a bullet against his back, and turned in anger. *Another ruined suit*, he seethed. He slowed his motorcycle and reached into the security car's passenger window. The cop fired wildly, but ROEBUCK grabbed his arm and pulled him from the car completely, dumping him onto the road. He rolled a few times after falling to the pavement. Tires screeched behind him, and he pushed himself up from the road, bloody but alive.

The car's driver cut the wheel and rammed into ROEBUCK's motorcycle. ROEBUCK spun behind the car, and did his best to keep balanced. The effort was futile. His motorcycle landed on top of him after his tire struck the curb. He pushed the bike up, brushed himself off, and continued after them, but Baxter and the police were blocks ahead by then.

Baxter turned around in his seat and fired at the pursuing car, difficult with the passenger clutching his back. The car swerved to avoid the bullets, but one of Baxter's shots still shattered the windshield. He could see the cop's face, stung by broken glass, flushed with anger. Baxter couldn't see ROEBUCK any more. He hoped his partner had only fallen behind and not been destroyed.

His revolver was empty by then, so Baxter swapped it for his nine millimeter. Behind him, the car came menacingly close, inches from his bumper. Another cop fired from the back seat, but his aim failed. Bullets whizzed past. Baxter turned around and fired a couple more shots. He shattered the car's rear window, but didn't hit either of the security cops. But he noticed the man in the backseat had stopped firing, and guessed he'd run out of bullets or needed to reload.

Baxter slowed the bike and let the car run alongside him. They'd reached a relatively empty area of Slate Street, so the traffic had thinned out. Baxter fired into the backseat. He felt the woman's face bury into him. The backseat cop raised his hands reflexively, and Baxter saw the ring finger on the man's left hand fly off in a small explosion of blood and bone.

The cop screamed, pained and enraged, and sprayed blood on the driver. The driver looked back, but at the wrong moment. He almost slammed into a car stopped in front of them, and swerved to avoid it. The car spun out, and in this moment of distraction, Baxter led his motorcycle down a side street away from the police.

"Where are we going?" the woman asked.

"We need to find ROEBUCK," Baxter told her.

"Who's that?"

"My bot."

"Oh. Him. Yes, I've seen him before. I know him."

* * * * *

ROEBUCK leaned against a brick wall in a dark alley. It was night. The stars' luminosity was intense. Orion's belt shone overhead near the waning moon. Sirens wailed in the distance, but no security patrol would venture this deep. *I hope he charged his radio*, ROEBUCK thought. "Baxter, this is ROEBUCK. Come in."

"ROEBUCK? You okay?" Baxter's voice came back through the radio with more than its usual rasp.

"Yes. Can you meet me back at the hotel?" ROEBUCK asked.

"Ten-four, good buddy. Over and out." Baxter answered.

"Over and out," ROEBUCK repeated. He climbed on his bike and got on a road that paralleled Slate Street and led back to his hotel. ROEBUCK had software that allowed him to detect vehicles broadcasting police and military radio frequency. It made them easy to avoid.

He sped his bike, a sleek Japanese model painted black and gun-metal grey, through the streets. To some of the drivers, he appeared as nothing more than a streaking red light flashing by them. His engine hummed high and loud, creating a Doppler effect for pedestrians. To him, the hum was constant so he forgot about it. Only the blur of the cars mattered, but with his computer calculating speeds and trajectories, apart from his human companion, he could speed through the night's traffic with a machine's precision.

The hotel's neon light glowed. A cool green beacon of hospitality. ROEBUCK parked his motorcycle. Baxter's stood nearby. He walked to their room and knocked. The hotel's owner had only given them one key, so he had to wait. Baxter let him inside.

"Good to see you," Baxter told him. "This here's Doc D'Angelo. She knows you."

"A doctor?" ROEBUCK asked.

"A Ph.D. I hold a doctorate in computer engineering. I helped reactivate you," D'Angelo explained.

"Reactivate me?" ROEBUCK asked. "What do you mean?"

"You were found. Two hundred years ago in the desert near Roswell, New Mexico. Your grey companions died at impact, but you were easy to preserve. Eventually, our technology caught up with you, and we were able to reverse engineer the aliens' tech and figure out how to wake you. I think you were their pilot and bodyguard," D'Angelo explained. "At least, that's what the generals told us. I think they wanted to turn you into a weapon."

"Did you work in Los Alamos?" Baxter asked.

"For a time. That's where our facility was located. Then the subject disappeared. We tried to recreate you, but were unsuccessful. We were abused. Starved. Beaten. 'Motivation,' they told us. I escaped. But they tracked me down in Rock Springs. That's where I ran into you two," D'Angelo explained.

"How serendipitous. A bit too serendipitous for my taste," ROEBUCK suggested suspiciously. "Are you some kind of trap?"

"No!" D'Angelo gasped. "Why would I put myself in so much danger?"

"To gain our trust. Lead me back to your minders," ROEBUCK told her. "How can we know you're telling the truth?"

"You'll have to believe me," D'Angelo said, "if you want your memories back."

"ROEBUCK, what's she talking about?" Baxter asked.

"You know how I told you I couldn't remember anything before you found me?" ROEBUCK reminded him. "I told you my memory was damaged. That it might come back. I was lying. It had been erased. I didn't want to think about that, so I made up a lie. To try to convince myself. It never worked, of course. But somehow, it made it easier."

"The scientists who found you, they accessed your memory," she explained. "That's how they understood your technology. Only they didn't want you to remember what happened when it was time for you to wake you up. So they erased it from you. But they didn't destroy it. It's still there, in Los Alamos."

"What do you think, ROEBUCK?" Baxter asked. "Ready for a home-coming?"

ROEBUCK flickered an affirmative. "Into the hornet's nest? I guess we must."

"I know a way in," D'Angelo told him. "It'll be dangerous, but not impossible."

"Par for the course," Baxter said.

"It's time to remember what I forgot."

Episode II:
The Flood

The rain fell over everything. It slid down the curves of every smooth rock and blighted tree. Each footprint formed a puddle. Baxter looked up from the muddy ground into the gray slate of the clouds. Their thick, saturated mass covered the sky and bled onto the earth.

His ankles were submerged. Then his knees. Baxter climbed onto the roof of a car. The town was washing away. Bits of garbage and refuse followed the flood's current like a tiny flotilla. In a canoe, ROEBUCK washed up next to Baxter's refuge. His black suit was soaked. The bot put his oar inside the craft, and held his hand out to Baxter. Baxter took it, gripping the cold, metallic fingers as he stepped off the car and into the canoe. The boat rocked as Baxter stepped inside, bearing his weight with a gentle bounce.

ROEBUCK began paddling as Baxter settled in. An ostrich looked up at them from the street, only its head and a few inches of skinny neck poking up from the surface. The storm waters pulled the canoe along a rapid torrent, until nothing else could be seen above its choppy waters except the tops of scraggly trees, a few stubborn leaves still clinging to their branches.

In the distance, a bolt of lightning forked the sky. Thunder rumbled, a loud and distant roar. Then the wave formed. A wall of water, sixty feet high, coming at them with grim inevitability. Some of the trees that stood in the wave's path were pulled from the earth and brought along the water's fury. As its crest reached their canoe, Baxter and ROEBUCK were picked up with it until they balanced upon its peak. The wave dipped, and Baxter looked down to see the water fold in on itself, he and ROEBUCK about to be caught between--

Baxter woke with a start. He sat up from the pile of clothes he'd gathered on the floor, a thin blanket falling from his chest. Doc D'Angelo looked down at him through the steam of her coffee cup.

"Not a morning person?" she asked.

"I had a dream," he told her. "About a flood. It was raining, and the water washed everything away. ROEBUCK found me, and brought me into a canoe he was paddling, but then we were caught up in a gigantic wave, and just when we were about to come back down from it..."

"You woke up," Doc D'Angelo finished for him. "I know the feeling. It's been a long time since I've had a good night's sleep."

"Got any more of that coffee?" Baxter asked.

D'Angelo handed him a steaming plastic mug. "Drink up. ROEBUCK says our caravan is leaving soon."

Baxter blew ripples into the coffee, took a sip, and wiped some of the sleep from his eyes. He stepped outside and saw ROEBUCK working on his cycle. The bot looked back at him. "Making some last minute adjustments. One of the tires came slightly out of alignment when I took that spill last night on Slate Street. It's fixed now. At least to a hundredth of a degree and well within the margin of error."

"Sounds good. I'll be ready in a minute," Baxter told him. "I need to go back inside for a sec and talk to the Doc."

"Make it quick," ROEBUCK said glancing behind him. "They're almost ready." Nearby, the other members of the caravan primed their vehicles for the voyage back. Already, engines revved one after the other in a primitive display of horse power.

"Be right back," Baxter told him.

He went into his hotel room to see Doc D'Angelo cramming a few meager possessions into her backpack. "Before we go," Baxter announced, "we need to get our story straight."

"What do you mean?" she asked, hooking her thumbs beneath the pack that rested on her shoulders.

"It won't do for people to know who you are. So we need to figure out a story for you."

D'Angelo nodded back at him. "To throw Corporate Security Force off my scent. So who am I? Some kind of long-lost aunt?"

"That'll do. You're my aunt Angela. And you're not a scientist," Baxter said, buttoning his shirt and pulling his sleeves through his leather jacket. "You're a school teacher. Coming back with us to look for work."

"Plausible," D'Angelo surmised.

"Alright, good. C'mon, we gotta go before we're left behind."

D'Angelo followed Baxter out the door. ROEBUCK sat on his cycle. He nodded, and rode toward the rest of the caravan. They surrounded the freighter that had brought fuel to Rock Springs. Now it was full of Rock Springs wheat to bring back to the distilleries.

Baxter followed him over. Lester looked out from the passenger seat of one his pick-ups. "Good to see ya, Baxter. Worried we'd have to leave you behind. Who's she?"

"Lester, this here's my Aunt Angie. She's a school teacher, coming back with us to help raise the little hellions back home," Baxter told him.

Lester looked at D'Angelo and nodded. "Just hold on tight. Might be a bumpy ride."

* * * * *

Doc D'Angelo gripped Baxter's torso and held on. *For dear life*, she thought to herself, *clichés be damned*. The desert's scenery sped by at nearly a hundred miles an hour. The horizon was fixed; blue sky over gray rock and the desert's deep brown. Closer, cacti and tumbleweed blurred. Nearly half a mile away, a jackrabbit glanced up at the speeding juggernaut of the freighter, thumped one its hind-feet a few times, and ducked into a small warren tucked underground.

A twinge of nausea flittered through D'Angelo's gut, so she took her eyes away from the road and burrowed her face into the back of Baxter's leather jacket. She wore a helmet borrowed from one of the other bikers in the convoy. He'd cracked the helmet he considered 'lucky', but D'Angelo decided it would be better than no protection at all, so she smashed it onto her stubborn curls, grown into a mass of tight corkscrews since her time on the run. *First things first: a haircut. Even if I have to shave everything off.*

The back of Baxter's jacket was warm and mostly smooth on her face. A few patches and stitches provided texture. Wind from the road whipped tears from her eyes. She wiped them off on the jacket, leaving behind slightly darker spots where the leather was moist. Her breath caught in the bandana she wore over her nose and mouth, but it kept the dust out, and that's all that mattered.

As the horizon blazed by, D'Angelo let her mind wander. She remembered the long days spent in cold, sterile laboratories and reflected on how far she'd come since then. ROEBUCK reminded her of the lab itself: cold, metallic, precise. Of course, the bot had been changed by his time outside the lab just as she had. *Escape. An independent variable if one ever existed.* A dozen what-if's flashed through her mind, but she was pleased with her new-found freedom. Even though her scientist's mind craved consistency, D'Angelo was glad she couldn't see any of the other possibilities that could have existed with her still trapped in the lab like any other mindless instrument. *Like a mouse in cage.*

The convoy began to slow. The feel of crunching gravel vibrated through the tires and into her body. Baxter leaned his bike over, and killed the ignition. The rest of the convoy did the same.

"Yeehah! We're back boys. Stand in line and get your scrip. Congratulations on a job well done," Lester roared to his men.

"Rather jubilant for one who lost some of his crew to an ambush," ROEBUCK remarked.

"You gotta think about the odds, ROEBUCK. Almost everybody came back from Rock Springs. We delivered our payload. Lost a few men to the raiders, but not the cargo or the whole escort. Gotta say, that's pretty damn good," Baxter told him.

"I understand ROEBUCK's point of view," D'Angelo remarked. "Some of us tolerate nothing but perfection."

"There's a recipe for unhappiness," Baxter said with a grunt.

* * * * *

Baxter and ROEBUCK parked their cycles, and went inside a rickety wooden office with a world-weary woman sitting behind a window. A circle had been cut from the glass for her to speak through; underneath there was a small space she used to slide paperwork.

When it was Baxter's turn, she told him in a tired monotone, "This scrip is good for one hundred Benny bucks at the Los Bonitos Distillery company store. It cannot be replaced. Thank you for your service to Los Bonitos." She placed a heavy red stamp on a square in one of the corners of the coupon and slid it through the window.

"Much obliged," Baxter said with a smile.

ROEBUCK got his share in just another moment. The pair walked outside to meet the Doc. "Scrip from the company store?" she asked with a smile. "Not much you can do with that if we're leaving town."

"That thought had crossed my mind. What should we do, Baxter? Save them?" ROEBUCK asked.

"Nah," he told them. "We'll exchange it. Might lose a bit of their value, but I prefer more universal currencies."

"And what would those be?" D'Angelo asked.

"Ammunition. Ethanol. Non-perishable food items. You know, the basic building blocks of life in this world we live in," Baxter explained.

With these words, the trio got back onto their bikes. They visited Mac near his ostrich burger hut. He was just closing up. "Hey, Baxter! You came just in time. Let me take you back to storage. Got a few things I'd like to show you."

Mac shared some of his unsold leftovers with Baxter and D'Angelo. D'Angelo ate hungrily. Baxter munched slowly, taking swigs from his water canteen and passing it back and forth to the Doc.

"Who's she?" Mac asked.

"This is my aunt Angie. Angie, this is Mac. He's an old friend. Angie's come back with us from Rock Springs to teach young'uns," Baxter explained.

Mac chuckled. "Good luck." He'd brought them back to what looked like a large, outdoor freezer. Inside, only a small compartment was actually refrigerated. The rest was full of armaments, ammunition, and black market ethanol. It was crowded inside, so only Baxter entered. ROEBUCK and D'Angelo waited outside the ostrich burger hut.

"Ninety bucks worth of nine millimeter bullets will do her just fine," Baxter instructed.

"I can do that for you. Got one more thing I want to show you before you make up your mind," Mac told him. He and Baxter carried out a couple ammo cases that could be carried on Baxter's and ROEBUCK's bikes.

"C'm'ere," Mac instructed. He brought Baxter back out and led him and the others toward an object of some size outside his storage shed "Saw you ride in on the back of Baxter's cycle," he nodded at D'Angelo. "If you have any more passengers, Baxter, this might come in handy." Underneath the canvas was a gleaming black sidecar. It had a comfortable looking maroon leather seat inside. ROEBUCK let out a low electronic whistle.

"Looks nice," Baxter said. "Might make her hard to maneuver."

"I wouldn't recommend it for combat," Mac told him. "Unless you add some armaments. That being said, it might make for more comfortable transportation for your passengers."

Baxter nodded. "I'll take it. If I don't like it, I'll trade it for something else."

"Excellent!" Mac said. He took a case of bullets back from ROEBUCK. "Pleasure doing business with you, Baxter."

"You too, Mac. And if it's all the same to you, don't mention my Aunt Angie to anybody that passes through," Baxter told him.

"My lips are sealed," Mac put a finger over his lips as if to quiet himself.

* * * * *

"Are we ready to get this show on the road?" ROEBUCK asked. "According to my internal navigation system, it's a long way to Los Alamos.

"We'll leave tonight," Baxter told him. "Camp on the road. Sound good to you, Doc?"

"A tent and a bedroll would be more comfort than I've been used to in a while. And it would be good to see the stars again. You're picking up idioms," she said to ROEBUCK. "Interesting.

Baxter grinned. "Alright, let's go."

D'Angelo put her hand on Baxter's wrist. "One minute. Do either of you cut hair?"

"I've barbered Baxter for the past couple years," ROEBUCK told her.

"Good," D'Angelo said. "Cut it all off."

"You're sure?" Baxter asked.

"I'm tired of these curls. Too damn hot under a motorcycle helmet. Besides, it's hair. It'll grow back," D'Angelo said.

"Give me a moment," ROEBUCK told them. He brought D'Angelo with him to a dark spot beneath a tree a few feet from the dusty street. Baxter sat on a curb next to Mac's and sipped on one of his beers.

ROEBUCK poured some water on D'Angelo's hair and ran his fingers through it. Even though his fingers were metal, ROEBUCK had a surprisingly human touch. For the bot, the experience was strangely intimate, especially since he didn't know the Doc near as well as he knew Baxter. He used one of Baxter's knives, a small switch blade, to cut her hair.

"I guess we put some barber code into your CPU before we reactivated you. You've got a nice touch," D'Angelo said quietly.

ROEBUCK let out a few electronic warbles D'Angelo took for laughter. "Baxter taught me how to do this. He was tired of using his mirror. He helps me with my own maintenance from time to time."

Once he'd chopped most of the hair from D'Angelo's head, ROEBUCK added some more water and a bit of soap. Then he began sliding the blade against her scalp. "Do you have a first name?" ROEBUCK asked.

"Doc," she told him. "I might tell you. Some day."

"Understood." ROEBUCK finished the haircut, leaving D'Angelo bald. Her pale scalp looked strange to him, but she placed her helmet back onto her head.

"Let's go.

The ride to their campsite was calm and easy. The sidecar worked well. D'Angelo relished seeing the landscape open up in front of her, and felt more secure buckled into the sidebar than she had clinging to Baxter. Mac gave her some goggles, so along with her new helmet (not that cracked, old relic she'd inherited from the caravan) and one of Baxter's bandanas, she felt much more suited to motorcycle travel.

ROEBUCK and Baxter rode alongside each other. Once the sun began to set, they found a good place to make camp. They didn't start a fire, just in case D'Angelo was still being followed. Instead, Baxter cooked a can of beans with his hot plate and a miniature propane tank. He shared the beans with D'Angelo. They washed their meal down with water from the canteens. Full and sleepy, she and Baxter collapsed onto their bedrolls while ROEBUCK stood watch.

* * * * *

Baxter must have had too much water with those salty beans, because his bladder woke him in the middle of the night. He sat up on his bedroll and looked up into the barrel of a gun pointed at him.

"Good morning, Baxter," a gruff voice spoke.

"Max. Good to see you," Baxter greeted him. "Leroy with you?"

"Leroy! Say hello," Max yelled behind him.

"Hey, Baxter!" Leroy spoke with an enthusiastic twang. His right arm held D'Angelo in a headlock; his left hand held a gun to her head. ROEBUCK stood nearby, but his optic sensors were dark. He was powered off.

"What did you do to my bot?" Baxter asked.

"E.M.P.," Max said.

"What the hell does that mean?"

"Electro-magnetic pulse," D'Angelo explained. "Deactivates electronics. Briefly."

"Shut up," Leroy dug the barrel of the gun into her temple.

Baxter leapt up as Leroy glanced back at his partner. In one quick movement, he grabbed Max's wrist, twisted his arm, and forced him to fire his gun in Leroy's direction.   The bullet fired wide. Leroy threw D'Angelo to the ground and aimed his gun at Baxter. Baxter tugged Max's gun from his hand, and hit him in the back of the head with the butt of his pistol.

He and Leroy locked guns in a stand-off. D'Angelo made a motion to stand up, but Leroy pulled another gun from his hip with his left hand and pointed it back at her. Baxter pulled his own gun and aimed it at Max, Max's gun still fixed on Leroy.

"How you want to settle this, amigo? This is your last chance. We can pretend this never happened, walk away friends." Baxter offered.

"Ain't gonna be that way, Baxter," Leroy spoke. He cocked the gun he had aimed at D'Angelo. "Drop 'em."

Beads of sweat peppered Baxter's brow. That E.M.P. had been a dirty trick. Maybe he could shoot Leroy first, take Max prisoner. *Leroy must be thinking the same thing*, Baxter thought. Beneath him, Max rolled on the ground, swept his feet around, and tripped Baxter's legs. Max put a knee into Baxter's gut, grabbed his gun back, and stripped him of his weapons, except for a boot knife that remained hidden under the cuff of his pants leg. *Sloppy*, Baxter silently critiqued, *but good for me*.

"Alright, Baxter," Max spoke. "You're a son of a bitch, but I can't blame you for trying. This lady and the bot are the only ones we've been hired to find. We'll let you go if you promise not to follow us. Have to keep your guns of course."

"Can't do that," Baxter spoke. "ROEBUCK and I been through hell together. And the Doc's important too."

"ROEBUCK?" Leroy asked.

"The bot," D'Angelo explained.

"I see," Max said. "Well, have to take us with you then. We got a couple pick-ups parked a half mile out. We'll take those cycles with us, should be good trade. But we'll come back for 'em. The bot'll be out cold for a couple more hours."

* * * * *

Baxter perked up when he saw the lights from the compound in Los Alamos. He'd been dozing, his head leaning against the passenger window, conserving his strength for the struggle he knew was coming. The facility was surrounded by a high security fence topped with coils of barbed wire. A search-light flooded the truck with an invasive beam that blinded Baxter, but Max honked his horn, and the light moved on.

Max and Leroy had known Baxter from years past. Once, they had all been in the same security police precinct, and deputized Baxter from time to time to help them hunt raiders. Eventually, they were fired for incompetence and excessive force in an illegal weapons raid that turned sour. Max and Leroy became mercenaries, like Baxter, often taking jobs Corporate Security Force were reluctant to do themselves.

Max and Leroy had become gloves when C.S.F. didn't want to get their hands dirty, so Baxter knew that was likely the reason they'd been sent after them after the chaos that erupted in Rock Springs when he'd first encountered the Doc.

Baxter peered out his window into Leroy's truck. D'Angelo still sat in the passenger seat next to Leroy. Each pick-up had a motorcycle in the back, including D'Angelo's side-car, still attached to Baxter's Harley. ROEBUCK was also tied down in the back of Leroy's truck next to his Kawasaki. *Was that a glimmer of red I saw in ROEBUCK's sensor?* Baxter wondered. *Wishful thinking, I bet.*

An armed guard came from the security gate and approached the vehicles. Max rolled down his window.

"Got an acquisition for the missing equipment and personnel report you released," Max explained as he passed a sheet of paper through his window.

The guard examined the document. He had an assault rifle strapped to his back, and wore black military fatigues with a short-billed cap. "Who's this guy?" He nodded in Baxter's direction. "And what's with the motorcycles?"

"This here's my prisoner. Captured in the course of our operation. The bikes are spoils of war," Max explained. "We'll trade 'em elsewhere if you ain't got use for 'em here."

Leroy held down his horn for a few seconds.

"Your buddy seems kind of antsy," the guard told him. "He alright?"

"He can be a little shit sometimes," Max conceded. "But it's to be expected. We been on the road for a hell of a long while, and ain't had the chance to unwind for too damn long. He's a little high-strung, that's all."

"Hmph," the guard grunted. "Better be on his best behavior inside. Major Monk don't put up with any shenanigans. But everything here looks in order." He waved them through, and the wooden arm of the security gate rose to admit them. Behind it, the compound seemed mostly empty. A few hangers stood here and there near some runways that seemed to stretch on forever. That was it. But then the road inside the base began to split, and a ramp formed, leading down into some kind of hidden subterranean compound.

"Never thought I'd be back here," Baxter grunted.

"Didn't know you'd been to Los Alamos," Max said.

"There's a lot you don't know," Baxter told him. Max ignored the provocation.

Leroy's truck followed them down the ramp into a bright, gleaming underground military facility, glowing with fluorescent light. A few troops were running drills in the massive space, at least a half a mile in length and width. Wide corridors split from this main space to other sections of the base. Some tanks, humvees and other military hardware shone under the lights. A few looked brand new. Even experimental. Most were pre-war, but well-maintained, even if they were more than a hundred years old.

A guard approached Max's window. "Park your truck here. Everybody out," he ordered. Max and Leroy parked their trucks and killed the ignitions. Guards led Baxter and D'Angelo from their seats. D'Angelo looked distraught, almost broken. At second glance, Baxter realized it was a ruse. There was hatred in her eyes, an intensity he'd rarely seen before. She met his glance for a moment, and Baxter understood her meaning: *'Help me, and I can get us out of here.'* Baxter nodded, ever so slightly.

An entire squad came into the bed of Max's pick-up and brought ROEBUCK down from the truck. A team of scientists had gathered, and one of them restored partial power to the bot to make him easier for them to move. They looked to be wearing the same kind of lab coat as Doc D'Angelo, but of course theirs weren't torn and tattered. A few soldiers led D'Angelo and ROEBUCK away with the scientists. Another guard approached Baxter, Max and Leroy.

"The Major wants to see you," he announced. "He needs to decide what to do with the prisoner."

"Understood," Max nodded.

Max and Leroy followed the guard down one of the corridors, bringing Baxter along with them. Baxter still wore Max's handcuffs. The guard knocked on a wooden office door emblazoned with the seal of a white eye staring out from a black pyramid. "Come in!" a voice barked from inside. The guard led them in, saluted the Major, spun on his heel and stepped outside, letting the door close behind him.

"Uncuff him, boys," the officer commanded. He was a thin, bald man with a horseshoe of brown hair wrapped around his skull and eyes that seemed locked in a perpetual squint. He wore a heavily decorated officer's uniform of olive and khaki, covered in medals and insignia. He gave Baxter a squinty glance, then his eyes widened in a double-take. "I remember you. You're that sum'bitch stole the bot in the first place, ain't ya?"

"Guilty as charged," Baxter admitted.

"Hell boy, I don't know whether to kill you or hire you," the man roared with a grin. "I'm Major Monk. What's your name?"

"Baxter," he said.

"Just Baxter?" Monk asked.

"I don't know my dad, and my mom only ever called me Baxter," he explained.

"We only ever called him Baxter, sir," Leroy told him.

"You know this man?" Monk asked.

"He used to partner with us from time to time. Deputized him into a few posses. We're ex-C.F.S. After we got canned, we'd still get contracts from time to time, under the table. Baxter helped us with a few of those," Max explained. "But we ain't seen him before tonight coming on five years now.

"Damn, son," Major Monk squinted at Baxter, "you got one hell of a reputation. I'll tell you what, boy. I'm going throw you in the brig, and in the morning, we'll have a little fun with you. Then I'll decide what to do next. Guard!" he yelled.

The same guard who escorted Baxter into the office came back in to retrieve him. He brought Baxter to his feet and cuffed him again.

"You boys can bunk here if you'd like," Monk offered. "Got some spare beds in the barracks. And help yourselves to the Mess. Requisitions Officer will compensate you for your troubles."

"Much obliged, sir," Max said with a nod.

The guard took Baxter out into the hallway and began walking him down a different corridor than Max and Leroy. Baxter leaned his head toward the guard, and spoke conspiratorially, "Word to the wise, kid. It's about to get real ugly. I'd fake a stomach ache, lock yourself in the infirmary."

The guard scowled, but said nothing. At the end of the hallway, he opened a barred cell and pushed Baxter inside. "Keep your eyes on that wall," he ordered.

Baxter obeyed. He heard the click of the handcuffs, and in one swift motion, brought a hoop of the metal bracelets into the man's temple. The guard stumbled backward. As fast as a cobra, Baxter had his boot-knife in the guard's throat. "Tried to warn you, kid," Baxter whispered as the man's eyes rolled back into his head as a second bloody grin seeped blood down his neck.

He stripped the guard of his uniform, and stuffed his own clothes into a canvas bag he'd found folded up in a nearby closet in the outside hallway. Baxter examined himself in the cell's mirror, a metal square that offered a warped reflection of his grizzled face. "Won't pass a close inspection. But maybe I can sneak into the lab."

* * * * *

Major Monk paced back and forth in front of the scientists he'd assembled in the Robotics Lab. "We've gathered today to welcome our prodigal Doctor D'Angelo back into our fold. Doctor Dee, welcome back," he winked as he said this. "I understand why you left. It was my fault. I pushed you too hard. Your brilliant minds are simply too fragile and I've been cruel. That's why I'm increasing your rations by twenty-five percent. And you'll be getting the good stuff. Canned pineapple with your spam, the freshest ostrich meat, and apple juice full of vitamin C. I've made your schedules more flexible to give you time for rest and socialization. Our Pleasure Officer has even offered full use of her Morale Corps in whatever capacity you see fit."

"What I'm trying to say is, we want you to be happy. Doctor D'Angelo, I can't tell you how terribly our research has suffered in your absence. It wasn't your fault ROEBUCK was taken from us, and I shouldn't blame you for not being able to help us build a new bot. Hell, ROEBUCK's creators must have had a few hundred million years of evolution on us! But now he's back, you're back, and our little project can continue. Under my supervision, of course."

"ROEBUCK, I know you can hear me. Your aural sensors and CPU have been momentarily reactivated so that you can understand my offer. You'll have your own privileges. Access to research materials. Time outside. You can even show us some of those tricks you learned on that Jap bike you brought back with you. I want you all to know," Monk said to the assembled scientists and their subject, "that my generosity comes with one condition. If my good will does not earn results, you'll begin losing these new privileges one by one. And if I am betrayed, I'll kick you out into the desert for you to fend for yourselves. You can fight the coyotes for your dinner. Or you can stay here with me. And I promise, once we have a working bot comparable to ROEBUCK, he'll have his companion and you can all retire. You can go wherever you want to, or stay here with us."

The scientists nodded quietly. Doctor D'Angelo stood with a quiet fury in her eyes the Major found unsettling, but the rest appeared cowed. "Good. Doctor D'Angelo, a word. The rest of you, get back to work!"

D'Angelo approached Major Monk as the other scientists returned to their experiments. "Yes, sir?" she asked with cold formality.

"You've been with the subject. How is he?" Monk asked.

"He's...different. He's learned so much. And I don't think we'll be able to keep him under our control for very much longer," D'Angelo warned.

"Leave that to me."

* * * * *

ROEBUCK woke slowly to full awareness. He felt his circuits fire one by one. His optic sensor powered on. Above him, a blank ceiling with fluorescent lights glowed white. He concentrated energy on his bio-sensors, but there was too much activity in the base, so he couldn't find Baxter. Dr. D'Angelo was near him, her pulse steady, blood pressure slightly elevated. *Alert. Good.*

ROEBUCK's amplifiers played a recording from the library of music stored inside of him. *"Been away so long I hardly knew the place! Gee, it's good to be back home. Leave it 'til tomorrow to unpack my case, honey disconnect the phone. I'm back in the U.S.S.R.! You don't how lucky you are, boy. Back in the U.S., back in the U.S., back in the U.S.S.R.!"*

"What the hell kind of commie propaganda is that?!" Major Monk snapped.

"Mid-20th century rock and roll music. He's well-versed," D'Angelo explained.

"Very well," Monk sighed, reluctant to surrender even a shred of his generosity, "but turn it down, godammit."

ROEBUCK turned the music down. Monk made a curt nod. D'Angelo came over to ROEBUCK, still lying prone on the table. She grasped ROEBUCK's fingers, her hand shielded from Monk's view. ROEBUCK felt her touch, and coiled his fingers ever so slightly. Inside his circuits, he felt warmth, a warm, maternal happiness that came from the Doc. She pretended to inspect him with a small magnifying glass. ROEBUCK felt her gaze into his optic sensor. He was able to see deep into D'Angelo's eyes, through her pupils, into her lenses, tangled forests of capillaries.

"I'm going to make a few repairs on ROEBUCK. He's incurred some damage in the field. I'll need access to my instruments," D'Angelo explained.

"Fine, fine," Monk replied. "Do whatever you need to, but no funny business. I have other duties to attend to. Let me know as soon as there are any breakthroughs."

"Yes, sir," D'Angelo replied.

ROEBUCK remained immobile, though his systems were fully restored. The E.M.P. Max used interrupted some of his functions, but only for a short time. *Where did a pair of drifters get access to that kind of tech? From Los Alamos, of course. So C.S.F. has melded with the remnants of the American military. I must remember that.*

D'Angelo put the magnifying lens near his aural sensor, a very small hole where a person's ear would be. To an observer, the hole would appear as a pin prick, but the sensitivity of ROEBUCK's instruments made him a superior listener compared to humans, and most other life-forms for that matter. Only bats and dolphins could rival his auditory skills.

"I know you can hear me," D'Angelo whispered. ROEBUCK felt her breath against his face. "We need to get out of here. And once we're gone, we'll run far, far away."

ROEBUCK beeped an affirmative. One of the other scientists glanced over. "His systems are still coming back online. The beeps are an auditory indicator."

She continued, "Baxter will be trying to escape. If he doesn't come for us within the week, you and I'll break out of here together or die trying."

"BOOOOOOooooooooop."

* * * * *

Baxter walked down the Los Alamos hallways with narrowed eyes and a clenched jaw. *Act like you belong here*, he told himself. He still had the duffel bag hanging from his left shoulder. He kept his right side clear in case he needed to fire the rifle, a 21st century assault model that seemed to be standard issue for the armed soldiers on the base.

The doors to the robotics lab stood closed. No guards were nearby. *Good. I'm in time. Once the body's found, the alarm'll sound, and I'll need to shoot my way out. If I'm not in the lab by then, D'Angelo and ROEBUCK will have to fend for themselves.* Baxter made these mental calculations as he stood outside the metallic sliding doors of the lab.

He held the guard's access card up to the door's sensor. The sensor glowed red for a brief moment. The door didn't open. *Guess knocking is out of the question.* Baxter studied the door's sensor and keypad. If ROEBUCK were here with him, he' hack into the electronics and have them inside in a matter of seconds. It frightened him how much he'd come to rely on his partner. If he lost ROEBUCK, he'd be just another gunslinger. Maybe he'd have to cut it as a mechanic. *Enough. Can't think like that. Not yet.* Baxter studied the door, as if the answers were woven in the steel.

Then suddenly the doors parted with a mechanical hiss, and a man in a lab coat walked outside. Baxter hurried through the open doors. "Hey, you can't go in without authoriz—" but the scientist's words were cut off as the doors shut behind him. Baxter hit a button near the lab's entrance to activate the mechanical lock.

All the scientists inside the laboratory paused what they were doing and looked in his direction. Even the music coming from ROEBUCK's speakers stopped with the sound of a skipping needle. *Wise-ass.* Baxter beamed the thought in the bot's direction. "Dr. D'Angelo. Major Monk wants ROEBUCK in his office, pronto. You need to bring him."

D'Angelo heard Baxter's familiar voice and recognized his disguise. ROEBUCK perked up too, sitting up from the examination table. "We'll be conducting some field-tests, so we'll be gone for a day or two. Bring your things," he ordered.

"Wait just a god-damned minute," a dark-skinned man with close-cropped hair stood up from his work. He was older than Baxter, probably in his sixties, but he carried himself with the confidence of a man half his age. "Dr. D'Angelo and ROEBUCK only returned an hour ago. I'm Chief Scientist in the robotics laboratory. Why didn't Major Monk clear this with me? I have important experiments scheduled for tomorrow. ROEBUCK needs to be here. Dr. D'Angelo too."

"You'll have to take that up with the Major, sir. I'm just following orders," Baxter told him. D'Angelo already had her backpack hanging from her shoulders, while ROEBUCK stood next to her, naked and gleaming.

"Let me see your requisition report," the chief demanded. "I'm not authorized to let any equipment leave the lab without signing it. I'll need to keep a copy too."

"I didn't receive one, sir," Baxter explained. "I'll have the Major send it as soon as I get back to his office."

"No," the chief said. "I'm calling Major Monk right now. You're not going anywhere." He began to reach for his phone.

Baxter pulled up his rifle and aimed from his hip. "That ain't a good idea, chief. You pick up that phone, things'll get real messy."

The man's eyes widened for a moment, and he sat down. "Very well. But I won't be bullied. Your days of strong-arming us are over. Even Major Monk says so."

Baxter lowered his rifle and tipped his hat in the scientist's direction. "Much obliged. I'll bring the doctor back with ROEBUCK in a few days. And I'll make sure the requisition order is delivered retroactively."

"Hmph. Very well.   But I don't like this one bit. This whole deal has a stink about it. Like some catfish left on the counter overnight." He peered at Baxter above his reading glasses.

Baxter gave him a half-hearted salute, unlocked the door, and led ROEBUCK and Doc D'Angelo back into the hallway outside of the lab. "ROEBUCK, nearest exit? There's a body in my cell, ain't wearing these clothes no more. "

"Calculating," ROEBUCK said. For a few moments, his optic sensor flared a bright ruby. "There is an access panel to a garbage chute located sixty feet north of this section of the corridor. It leads to a compactor that has access to the sewage system. It'll be the easiest way to avoid personnel."

"Is that safe?" Dr. D'Angelo asked.

"Safer than staring down a few dozen armed guards," Baxter said. "Let's go."

ROEBUCK led them down the corridor, his feet clanking on the metal floor. D'Angelo and Baxter followed him. As Baxter predicted, an alarm began to howl when they were only a few dozen feet from the lab's exit. Red light flooded the corridor, spinning from a couple siren bulbs placed at each end of the hallway.

"We're here," ROEBUCK announced. He stood in front of the access panel, pointing at it with his right hand. The bot's fingertip separated along a horizontal crease, and the end of a screwdriver emerged. As ROEBUCK studied the bolts, the end of the screwdriver changed subtly until it matched the size and shape of the gaps in the bolts that held the panel to the wall. He placed the end of the screwdriver into the first bolt, and it began to spin, unscrewing the bolt from the wall. They clattered on the floor, one by one, until the panel slid open.

ROEBUCK nodded to his companions, climbed into the open chute and slid down headfirst. He ended up in a pile of muck and waste, rusted military hardware, spent motor oil, empty glass bottles, and old fruit and vegetable peels. Baxter slid down behind him, grunting as he collided with the bot's hard exterior, and again a moment later when Doc D'Angelo fell on top of him.

"Get up!" Baxter said as he pushed her off. She rolled over into a puddle of grease and cursed. ROEBUCK lit a bright cone of red light from his optic sensor so his human companions could see in the darkness. "Okay, ROEBUCK, where the hell are we?" Baxter asked.

"We're in one of the garbage compression chambers." ROEBUCK explained. "The solid waste is compressed, and any liquid falls through the floor grates into the sewers below."

"We need to get the hell out of here then," Baxter said. "We didn't exactly close the door behind us. And it's only a matter of time before that open access panel is discovered. If we're still down here when they find it…well, we'll all be a lot skinnier, that's for damn sure."

"Agreed," D'Angelo spoke as she attempted to wipe the muck from one of the sleeves on her lab coat.

"Here's the exit," ROEBUCK pointed to a rusted metal door with a spinning wheel handle attached to it. "This leads to some steps that go down to the sewer system." The bot reared back on his left leg, and kicked the door with his right. The battered door flew off its hinges and clattered down a few concretes steps. "Poor structural integrity," ROEBUCK explained as he walked through the open portal. "Oxidation with the iron in the door. Common in a moist environment."

Baxter nodded as he followed ROEBUCK through the portal. D'Angelo crept behind them. They walked down the concrete steps and found a flowing river of waste leading through the sewer tunnels. Fortunately, narrow concrete walkways followed the waste through the tunnels, so they wouldn't have to slog through it. But the smell was impossible to avoid.

"More olfactory interference," ROEBUCK complained.

"Ain't exactly a spring meadow, but if it gets us out alive, that's all that matters."

*　*　*　*　*

"Here," Baxter handed D'Angelo one of his spare pistols. "You shouldn't be unarmed. Just in case we run into anything unexpected. You ever fire one of these before?"

"Never had the need to until very recently," D'Angelo said. "Point and pull the trigger, right?"

"That's the basic idea. Hold the gun straight in front of you. Both hands, like this." He molded D'Angelo's hands and fingers around the grip and trigger of the gun as he stood behind her. "Line up your target in the sight. Keep a tight grip; you'll feel a kick. Make sure the safety is off before you try to fire," Baxter explained. "Keep this lever up," he said as he indicated the safety on the pistol D'Angelo now gripped, "until you're ready to use it. Push it down when you want to fire. Or any time you think you might need to."

D'Angelo nodded and tucked the pistol into the waist of her pants. The gun was cold and heavier than she expected it to be. She brought her hand up to run her fingers through her hair only to find that the curled bush she was used to was gone; only the sandpaper of her shaved scalp remained. D'Angelo brought her mind back to the moment. Her eyes followed the beam of light ROEBUCK cast in front of them.

"How much further?" Baxter asked.

"Shouldn't be more than a mile. The sewage lets out into a creek bed outside the base," ROEBUCK explained. "One moment." The bot stopped so suddenly, Baxter almost walked into him. "Electronic interference. Coming from behind us. Fast. And large. More than one. They may be vehicles."

"We need to take cover. Try to stay out of the way, Doc," Baxter yelled behind him.

"You don't need to tell me twice," D'Angelo called back. She flicked the safety's lever just in case.

ROEBUCK leaped over the guardrail of the walkway they'd been travelling on, over the sewer's tunnel and onto the opposite concrete path. He transformed his right arm into its Gatling-gun form and aimed in the direction of the pursuers he'd detected. On the other side of the tunnel, Baxter knelt in a crouch with his rifle aimed back toward the path they'd followed. D'Angelo hunkered beside him, and peered through the guardrail, gripping her pistol with white knuckles.

The hum of motors grew, their rumbling cacophony amplified by the hollow tunnel. A white light blinded them, and in the next moment, bullets flew and chipped concrete bit into Baxter's hands and cheeks. He fired his assault rifle in the direction of light speeding down the tunnel. The guns firing at them stopped, and a blur of machinery flew past.

Baxter could see a pair of skids beneath a low-flying vehicle hovering above the water. There was a miniature jet engine in the rear of the craft that propelled it above the sewer. An inert propeller hung from the craft just below the engine. *Must be amphibious*, Baxter thought. As it turned around, he could see the craft was small, about the size of his own motorcycle. A pilot sat enclosed in a framed glass canopy. Doors enclosed this space. A deep olive metal frame protected the machinery underneath. An identical vehicle also maneuvered the tunnel and now both were headed back in their direction. Machine guns mounted beneath their cockpits fired at them again.

ROEBUCK and Baxter returned gunfire as the machines zoomed by. Glass shattered and sprayed behind them in a bright, glittering plume. "Yeeeeehah!" one of the pilots roared as he turned the craft around.

"Sounds like Leroy," Baxter grunted. D'Angelo was quiet beside him, but peered over the guardrail as the machine turned back.

As the trailing craft was about to fly past, ROEBUCK jumped from his side of the walkway and gripped the vehicle from its starboard skid. The vehicle rocked to the side as he held on, and the pilot pulled back on his stick to bring the craft level to rise higher above the water. It rose a few feet, but ROEBUCK's legs still dangled in the muck. He pulled himself up onto the skid and ripped open the cockpit's door. The pilot roared in alarm and fury, but ROEBUCK threw him out into the sewer. The craft veered down for a moment, but ROEBUCK pulled back on the control stick to regain its balance and commandeered control.

"Stay here. I'll be right back," Baxter told D'Angelo. He lowered himself from the walkway and into the muck. He lit a flashlight attached to the barrel of his rifle. It cast an eerie spotlight on the sewer's rippling surface. He wanted to know what had happened to the pilot ROEBUCK threw from the craft.

Baxter's gun-light reflected on the dark sewage, but other than the languid flow of the water itself, he couldn't detect any kind of movement. But as he scanned the water, a few bubbles finally emerged from the depths of the muck. Baxter kept beam of his gun's light fixed on one of the bubbles that trailed along the current.

From beneath the muck, a pair of arm's erupted from the water, and in a fraction of a second, Baxter was on his back, the pilot on top of him, pinning him down beneath the rifle which Baxter and the pilot each had a grip on.

"I'm gonna finish you off for good this time, Baxter!" the pilot spat through the grime coating his face. Baxter couldn't hear Leroy's voice, but had recognized him even under all the filth that covered him. *Max must be on the craft ROEBUCK is chasing*, Baxter thought. He grunted as struggled to push Max away from him while still holding onto the gun, and gasped as he got his head above the water.

In one moment of tremendous effort, Baxter shoved Max off and wrenched the rifle away. He aimed his gun, but before he could pull the trigger, he felt a thunderous pain in his temple that spread through the rest of his skull. Baxter's vision went black, as if his head had been dunked into an inkpot, and his mind surrendered itself to oblivion.

* * * * *

D'Angelo watched Baxter's fight with Max from the darkness of the walkway. She recognized Leroy's voice, and knew the man from their ride into Los Alamos together. He'd been driving the pick-up that had brought them into the base. Now Max stood over where Baxter had fallen into the water, reaching into the shallow muck to pull the rifle from him.

"Back off!" D'Angelo roared, her pistol aimed at Max. Her hands were shaking slightly, but they were both holding the gun. Max was lined up in her sight, just as Baxter told her.

Max looked up at her with a grin. He brought his hands out of the muck and held them up. Then he began to walk toward her.

"Lady, you might hurt yourself with that gun. Don't look like you're used to it. Why don't you hand it over so nobody gets hurt?" Max stretched his left hand out to her. His right hand crept behind his back.

"Not another step closer!" D'Angelo yelled. "Not another step!"

Max's grin transformed into an angry scowl, and he lunged at D'Angelo with a crowbar he'd hidden behind his back. D'Angelo pulled the trigger. The kick of the gun pushed her back and the flash of the muzzle nearly blinded her. She kept at it until the gun's clip was empty, the boom of the shots followed by the hushed click of an empty chamber.

Max's momentum carried him forward, so he fell facedown at her feet. D'Angelo was stunned for a moment, silenced in disbelief, until she noticed the smoky haze of the exit wounds and the pool of blood that spread out beneath the body.

* * * * *

ROEBUCK flew back into the sewer's entrance, his metal body pocked in places from the shrapnel of Leroy's grenades, scorched from the flames and smoke of the explosions. Damage was superficial. The blackened areas were mostly scorched carbon from dust and matter that had collected on his body's surface. The shrapnel's small dents looked as if a child had thrown a handful of pebbles into a figure made from sand. ROEBUCK rather liked the effect his battle-scarred body presented. It would intimidate most humans, and the feeling of nakedness he had inherited from his companions had been replaced by the robes of war.

Leroy'd made it out alive. ROEBUCK would've chased him out into the desert for the sake of tying loose ends, but his aural sensors had detected gunshots from inside the sewer. That meant Baxter and D'Angelo could be alive, dead or dying depending on who fired those shots. And if ROEBUCK could provide triage, which he had been programmed for in Los Alamos (and probably even before if D'Angelo's speculations were true), then it was his responsibility to save them.

The light from the tunnel's exit slowly dimmed behind him, and ROEBUCK found Baxter and D'Angelo where he'd left them. Baxter's head had a knot near his temple nearly three centimeters in diameter. D'Angelo was peering into his eye with a small flashlight she'd brought with her kit from the lab. She frowned slightly as she watched his pupils dilate and constrict.

"He appears to be concussed," D'Angelo said without looking up at the bot.

ROEBUCK made a cursory analysis of his vital signs. Still strong, but thrumming with the effects of adrenaline, cortisol and endorphins. "Do you mind?" he asked in a gentle voice.

D'Angelo stepped aside. She was still numb from the gunshots. The fact that she'd fired in self-defense salved her conscience, but barely. *I killed a man. And crossed a line. Eat or be eaten. The law of the jungle. That's the world I inhabit now.*

"He'll recover," ROEBUCK spoke. "But we need to leave. Immediately. They know we're down here."

"Agreed," D'Angelo said.

Baxter grunted an affirmative, and stood up, a bit wobbly at first. He leaned on ROEBUCK for a moment, sighed deeply, collected himself and looked down the sewer tunnel. "Shit."

The water was rising. Quickly. Its level rose a half a foot in about thirty seconds, as Baxter, D'Angelo and ROEBUCK clambered back onto the amphibious flying craft they'd stolen from Max. They sped away. ROEBUCK piloted the craft, and D'Angelo and Baxter each stood on one of the skids, hanging onto handles that were attached to the top of the cockpit's canopy for that very purpose.

It was all for naught. The gate outside the sewer tunnel was sealed, a metal portal completely closed so as to dam the water and flood the tunnel completely. ROEBUCK stopped the craft by turning it one hundred eighty degrees, and accelerating in the opposite direction until their momentum stopped. Of course, now they were facing the brunt force of the water head on.

"Hold on to me," ROEBUCK told Baxter and D'Angelo. "Don't let go. Take a deep breath and hold it for as long as you—"

EPISODE III:
RAMONA'S REVENGE

D'Angelo and Baxter gripped ROEBUCK with a clutching desperation as the bot stepped on the eject pedal and the canopy of the cockpit detached. He propelled himself up through the dank murk of the flooded sewer tunnel, but the ceiling wasn't very high, and no pockets of air remained to oxygenate his human companions.

ROEBUCK transformed to adapt to the aquatic environment. His feet elongated and webbed to resemble metallic flippers. They propelled him through the water faster than any human diver, but Baxter and D'Angelo still clung to him, the oxygen in their bodies diminishing with each precious second. ROEBUCK scanned for an alternate escape route, one that would take them into an un-flooded section of the base.

Eventually, he found it. Some barracks that had been decommissioned just a couple decades before the Great Fall. The shower facilities still had pipes leading to these very sewers, and even an old access port. Almost certainly sealed, but he had tools to deal with those kinds of obstacles. Like a fettered torpedo, ROEBUCK zoomed through the tunnels, clutching Baxter and D'Angelo behind him as he swam.

Meanwhile, Baxter's insides burned as he was pulled through the watered down river of shit. *Hell of a way to go*, he thought to himself, his head still aching from Max's strike. His eyes pinched, his mouth closed, his arm pulled by ROEBUCK, he remembered a prayer from his youth: *Hail Mary, full of grace, the Lord is with thee*. As the prayer went through his mind, he did not know the meaning behind it, but remembered a kind old lady from his boyhood, her wrinkled hands wrapped around beads, as she repeated this prayer over and over, and the comfort it gave him as she held him while they whispered it together. And so he shielded his mind and heart with this memory as his body swept through the flood.

D'Angelo knew no prayers to comfort her, but her mind was not still. *How much longer can I hold my breath? How much longer can*

ROEBUCK pull us through this muck before he's dragging two drowned corpses behind him? She felt a breath escape her lungs, but resisted the urge to breathe in, even though every cell in her body cried for air. Then she felt her arm tug up instead of forward, and even though she was being pulled in the darkness, she knew they'd changed direction.

ROEBUCK finally found the access port to those decommissioned barracks and rose up to meet it. The port was still sealed, but the bot knew that in the state of disrepair most of the abandoned sections of the base were in, he'd be able to break this seal if he could only create enough force and momentum. So he sped through the water as fast as he could, his feet fanning behind him like twin propellers.

At the moment of impact, ROEBUCK's head slammed into the metal seal and he pulled Baxter and D'Angelo along with him, like a submarine breaching ice to reach the ocean's surface. They collapsed on the floor of the barracks' washroom, D'Angelo and Baxter breathing in gulps of air, their faces' purple hue fading to red as they caught their breath. Their clothes were soaked and soggy, and they stank of waste, but at least they were alive.

ROEBUCK scanned for nearby life-forms. He also activated a dim light that emanated from the top of his head so that his companions could see inside the dark room.

"Anybody nearby?" Baxter asked.

"I sense one life-form that may be human. There's a lot of interference from vegetation, insects and small mammals. Certainly no groups of soldiers. They must assume we were destroyed when the tunnels were flooded," ROEBUCK said.

"That's good news," Baxter grunted, and winced in pain. "Damn, he really rung my bell. We'll want to keep our guard up."

"First things first," D'Angelo announced. "I need out of these clothes. Let's clean ourselves off. Here, this will help with the pain." She unscrewed the lid off a small plastic bottle. "Swiped this from one of the lab's first aid kits."

"Much obliged," Baxter said, then gulped, swallowing the capsule dry.

ROEBUCK opened a metal cabinet lined up against a wall. "Guard uniforms," he said. "They look a bit different than the ones the soldiers wear now. But at least they're dry."

"Thank heavens," D'Angelo said, and began stripping her wet clothes.

"You need some privacy?" Baxter asked.

"Don't be foolish," D'Angelo admonished. "This is no time for prudishness. Besides, we can't afford to separate. At least for now. And this shower's leaking. I wonder..." D'Angelo turned the shower's handle and laughed with glee as a stream of hot water poured out. She began to shed her soiled lab coat and the rest of her clothes.

"If you say so," Baxter said, peeling off his boots. In a few minutes, they wore dry, once black uniforms, now faded to a dark gray. Baxter's clothes fit well. D'Angelo's uniform was loose, so she rolled up her sleeves and pants, and tied a belt around her waist as tight as it would go.

"To the surface? "ROEBUCK asked. "We could steal a vehicle, maybe even our bikes, ride back into the desert."

"You sore we ain't found what we came come for yet?" Baxter asked. "Shame being this close to your memories, but not able to access them."

"Disappointing, yes," ROEBUCK said, "but not worth walking back into certain doom for. They'll be on high alert once they realize they're unable to find our remains."

"We may have another chance some other day," D'Angelo told him, placing a hand on ROEBUCK's shoulder. "That information is too valuable. They'll never get rid of it."

Baxter slid a magazine into a pistol, sliding it in with a soft click. "Looks like they left a few weapons behind too. Wonder what the hell happened here to make 'em leave in such a hurry. Here you go, Doc."

Baxter handed her a pistol. The weapons they had with them in the sewers remained there, lost in their escape. He led them to the barracks' exit. The door swung open with an ominous, metallic groan. The air hissed, and a colony of cockroaches skittered into cracks and crevices as ROEBUCK's light flooded the corridor. "Reminds me of my bachelor days," Baxter quipped. He walked through the doorway as ROEBUCK and D'Angelo came up behind him. Their scavenged pistols came with lights equipped, illuminating what lay ahead.

It wasn't much. Layers of mold and decay. Plenty of insects and vegetation, as ROEBUCK had detected. The smell of mildew and rot. Curiously, they even heard the skitter of pawed feet echo in the distance. "If there are animals down here, that must mean there's access to the surface," D'Angelo noted.

"Access to the surface, and angry den mothers both. Best to keep our guard up. We're intruders here," ROEBUCK reminded them.

Get out. Baxter felt a thought flash through his mind, but it didn't come from his own brain. It trod on his synapses like an unwelcome guest. *Get out!* the thought repeated more insistently. *Guns and soldiers aren't allowed here. I thought I made that clear.*

"Did anybody else hear that?" Baxter asked.

"Hear what?" said D'Angelo.

"I heard a voice in my mind. Telling us to get out. Haunted house shit," Baxter explained.

"I did detect a strong electro-magnetic signal directed at us. Feared it was from a scanning instrument. But an advanced telepath or telekinetic could be just as dangerous," ROEBUCK warned.

Baxter sighed. "If it ain't psychotic raiders or fascist soldiers, it's some subterranean, paranormal threat. When's it gonna end, ROEBUCK?" Baxter growled.

"When we retire, Baxter, voluntarily or involuntarily."

Baxter huffed, but kept quiet as the trio continued their search for a way to the surface. Down one of the tunnels, some kind of large rodent with beady red eyes hissed at them when they stepped a bit too close, but when ROEBUCK spun his Gatling gun in its direction and pointed his red targetting beam at it, the creature scampered off into the shadows.

I warned you. Baxter stopped in his tracks. "Get ready," he said. He cocked his pistol, and D'Angelo did the same. ROEBUCK spun his Gatling while they waited for an attack.

A whirlwind of metal and debris came spinning at them from the end of the corridor. Baxter and D'Angelo huddled into the recesses of a pair of doorways. ROEBUCK dug in his heels, crossed his arms in front of his face, and let the debris bounce off of him.

"Hey!" Baxter yelled down the corridor. "We're trying to get the hell outta here! We got drug down into this base by a couple of bounty hunters, but we're trying to escape. You help us outta here, or just leave us alone, we won't have to fight. You can keep the tunnels for yourself and those critters."

The whirlwind paused as if a calm in a storm.

A mass of tangled black hair descended from one corner of the hallway. A white eye peered out. Baxter stepped behind ROEBUCK, slowly and tentatively.

"We ain't soldiers, ma'am. Had to use these uniforms to replace the rags we *were* wearing. They flooded the sewer tunnels when we were trying to escape earlier. My bot here saved us from the waters, but the only place we could get to was up here in these tunnels with you. Beg your pardon, miss," Baxter had his gun tucked into the back of his waistband out of view. He held both his hands up with his fingers spread.

"I can tell you're not lying," the girl said. She spoke with a slight Mexican accent, not uncommon in these parts. She was wearing her own version of a soldier's uniform, cut and stitched into a tee-shirt and shorts with a green army jacket over-top. She had colorful cloth and materials, what looked like bandanas, tied into her clothes, along with a bright red bandana worn as a headband. In her right hand, she held a machete. It gleamed in the light coming from the guns. She also had infra-red goggles lifted onto her fore-head. Her skin was pale, but the girl look well-nourished. Despite her isolation, she'd seemed to take good care of herself.

"Who are you, little girl?" D'Angelo asked. "My name's D'Angelo."

"I'm fourteen. Not a little girl. But you can call me Ramona," she said, tucking her machete back into a leather loop she had on her belt. She held her hand out to D'Angelo who shook it, surprised by the girl's hard grip; compared to Baxter's firm handshake, the girl had fingers of granite.

"A pleasure to meet you, young lady," ROEBUCK said, bowing deeply with a flourish of his arms. "ROEBUCK, at your service."

155

"And I'm Baxter," Baxter said, with a gentle nod in the girl's direction. "You know the way out of here?"

"Of course I do," Ramona told him. "But if you want me as your guide, you need to pay up. Got any trade?"

Baxter cleared his throat, taken aback by the girl's assertiveness. "Well, let's see. The Doc and I scavenged a couple of pistol's. Think the Doc's got some medical supplies. And if you want to leave, we can take you with us. Least to the next town."

"Hmph," Ramona scoffed. "Well, I wouldn't usually help you in this kind of situation. I'm more of a 'kill first, ask questions later' kinda gal. But you've caught me in a generous mood. And it does get a little lonely in this base. Tell you what. I'll lead you up to the exit, and then decide what I'll do next. Just don't piss me off."

"Incredible," ROEBUCK remarked. "Neural implants. They augment an inherent psychic ability."

"Christ," D'Angelo swore. "I'd heard rumors of human trials. What did they do, kidnap a little girl and give her brain surgery?"

"I don't remember what they did to me," Ramona said. "I only remember waking up. And the experiments." A small shudder ran through her body. "But I decided my trial was over, and released myself under my own recognizance," she said happily, a malevolent gleam in her eyes.

"That sounds awfully familiar," ROEBUCK spoke. "Though I have no idea how one would remove memories from an organic brain."

"Hypnotic suggestion. Trauma. I hate to speculate further," D'Angelo said.

"Now that we've finished our introductions," Baxter told them, "we'd best be moving on. We're one search party away from a fire-fight."

"Yeah, yeah. Follow me. And try to keep up." Ramona led them back into the darkness. She gripped her machete, held at her side like an ancient tribes-woman, cutting through thick jungle.

Ramona's limbs were short, but strong. She had a stocky build, small and wide, but well-muscled. Her years in isolation hadn't seemed to impact her much, mentally or emotionally. She could still communicate. *Too well*, Baxter reflected. The girl certainly was opinionated, and had no problem telling them exactly what she thought. About the way they smelled (the stench of the sewers still clung to them), how slow and clumsy they were, and how stupid they must be to have been captured in the first place. Baxter wanted to give the girl a piece of his mind, but since she was their only way out of the base, felt it would be best to let her gripe, at least until they got to the surface.

"*HISS!*" Baxter backed up a step and aimed his pistol, but Ramona put a hand on his arm.

"It's okay, she's friendly," Ramona said, pushing Baxter's arm until his pistol pointed to the floor. She crouched low and sauntered over to the creature, clicking her tongue as she went. It was another one of those large, pale rodents with white hair and pink eyes. Ramona held something out in her hand that piqued its curiosity. The rodent sniffed curiously and took Ramona's offering, a dead cockroach she'd pulled from her pack. The possum stuffed the roach into its mouth and crunched greedily. Black flakes caught in the fur around its mouth, but the creature seemed happy now, and climbed up Ramona's arm to rest on her shoulder. It flicked its pink tongue out, licked its paw a few times, and began cleaning its face.

"What in tarnation...?" Baxter asked, scratching his head.

"Her name is Sandy. She's my possum," Ramona introduced her. "Helps me find food, water and warm places to sleep."

"Curious," ROEBUCK observed as Sandy groomed Ramona's hair.

"Doesn't appear to be rabid," D'Angelo remarked. "At least."

"Never heard o' no possum," Baxter said.

"Nocturnal creatures. Well suited to the darkness. They're usually seen as pests. They like to get in garbage. Mostly harmless. And very clever," ROEBUCK explained "They can even play dead."

"Ugly as sin," Baxter remarked.

"Like you should talk," Ramona scoffed.

Baxter sighed and rolled his eyes. "C'mon now, let's get. I want to see daylight."

Ramona led them through countless corridors as they made their way through the abandoned sections of the base. It seemed like they were in a maze of hallways, but with the girl leading them, they always knew where to turn, which steps to go up and down, and those areas best to avoid. Sometimes Baxter glanced down the paths they didn't take. Usually, he could only see an empty darkness, but every once in a while, a ceiling had caved in, or a pile of furniture or equipment blocked the way. Some loose wires shot sparks, sending flashes of blue light as they hissed and popped. Once or twice, he glimpsed some old bones. They poked out of piles of clutter, but whether they were human or animal, he never got close enough to see. *Don't matter now, I reckon,* he thought to himself as he pulled his eyes away.

"Let's stop here," Ramona announced abruptly. She pointed her machete at a pile of objects that looked more organized and intentional than the random heaps that had blocked off some of the other corridors. It almost looked like a den of sorts, with seat cushions, sleeping mats, curtains and clothing piled into a sort of nest.

As she made her way toward it, Sandy leapt from her shoulder head-first into a pile of clutter and came out with a startled mouse she'd grabbed with her paws. After a few frightened squeaks and frantic wiggling, Sandy put the creature out of its misery and gulped half of it down in a matter of moments. The mouse's tail hung from her mouth like a half-eaten spaghetti noodle.

"Pest control," Ramona giggled. She dug through a pile of clothing and opened up a sealed container, unhooking a couple of latches. Inside, there were rectangular pouches, neatly stacked, all sealed in plastic bags. "MRE's," she explained. "Meals ready to eat. I found a storage room full of these. Not too tasty, but they stay good pretty much forever. Here, I know you must be hungry," she said, tossing one to Baxter and another to D'Angelo. "Does he eat?" she asked, cocking her head at ROEBUCK.

"My energy comes from the sun," ROEBUCK explained. "And in these darkened tunnels, I'll only be able to power myself for about another hour or so."

"Eh, we'll be outta here in plenty of time," Ramona assured them. "Can't poke our heads out anywhere it would be too dangerous, ya know?"

Baxter grunted an affirmative, and crouched down in the corridor, leaning his back against the wall. He tore open the MRE with his fingers, and a few pouches fell out from the larger one.

"And how do we...?" D'Angelo asked, examining the packets that would become her meal.

"I just mix everything together," Ramona explained, grabbing a small metal bowl and placing it down in front of her. She passed some to Baxter and D'Angelo too, and began emptying the packets one by one into her own.

"Got it," D'Angelo said, following her lead. She tried not to look too hard inside the bowl. Even though it didn't look to have anything exactly growing inside of it, it wasn't perfectly clean either. Ramona poured some water from her canteen into D'Angelo's and Baxter's bowls.

"Now you just mix it up," Ramona explained. "There's a few different flavors of the goop. Never really bothered to read the labels too much after I got used to them. It's more fun if it's a surprise," she said, stirring the mixture with one of her fingers, and licking some of the mess.

"Hoo boy," Baxter said, but slurped the goop hungrily once he'd mixed it together. It tasted like salt and beef stock. A hint of carrots, maybe? And one clump that must've contained his dessert; it was a sweet mass of granulated sugar and artificial flavor. *But damned if I don't feel better*, Baxter thought. He was still a little hungry, but not terribly, and his mind felt a little sharper. He'd woken up a little.

D'Angelo and Ramona were careful to grab every speck of sustenance they could, running their fingers along the inside of their bowls and licking them clean. ROEBUCK looked on quietly. Baxter felt a twinge of worry. ROEBUCK's optic sensor grew dim, a red glow in the darkness, like the coals of a smoldering fire.

"We need to get to the surface," Baxter announced. "ROEBUCK ain't lookin' too good."

"I feel fine," ROEBUCK declared, "but my energy reserves will only last a little while longer. Then I'll power down."

"Yeah, yeah," Ramona said, chucking her metal bowl behind her into a darkened section of her den. She stood back up, grabbing her machete from the floor and slid It into a leather strap she wore on her hip. She raised her arms above her head as she stretched and yawned, then scratched at her belly. "Better get ready. We're not lucky, the shit's gonna hit the fan. I can take care of myself, but you guys better be careful."

"What do you mean?" D'Angelo asked as they began walking down the darkened corridor once more.

"I mean," Ramona explained, "Major Monk isn't going to be happy when he realizes his prize specimen got up and walked out of his lab. For a second time."

"How do you know the major?" asked ROEBUCK.

"We have a history," Ramona spoke in a low voice. "Let's just leave it at that."

"What did he do to you?" D'Angelo asked.

"I don't want to talk about it," Ramona ended the conversation with an edge in her voice even sharper than her machete.

D'Angelo quieted, and they continued walking. They crept through more abandoned tunnels, filled with a dank green mold, trickles of running water, and even more subterranean animals. Just as ROEBUCK looked about to tip over at any moment, Ramona put her hand on the rung of a metal ladder that led a few feet up into a manhole cover.

"We're here," she told them. "I'm going to go up and take a peak."

When she was halfway up, Baxter asked, "You want a gun?"

"I don't need one," she called back down. As she reached the top, she pressed her palm onto the metal above her and began sliding the manhole cover away. The sound as it scraped against concrete was like the growl of a hungry beast. Ramona poked her head out into the open portal as a beam of light parted the darkness of the tunnels. "Damn it!" Ramona cursed, pulling her head inside as she slid the manhole cover back. The tunnel darkened as they heard bullets ricochet off of it.

Ramona grit her teeth, and the manhole lid shot up like a champagne cork. The girl leapt from the tunnel with an impressive agility, and the sound of gunfire roared from above them.

"We have to follow her!" D'Angelo gasped.

"You're right," Baxter said. "Ain't gonna get a better distraction than that." He gripped the ladder's rungs and began scrambling up. D'Angelo followed close behind, with ROEBUCK coming after her.

Baxter climbed in a hurry, scrambling out onto the dusty surface. A howl and pinging of countless bullets surrounded and consumed him. He huddled behind some metal storage crates piled about three feet high, and knelt behind them to view the chaotic scene.

Ramona had tripped an alarm when she'd removed the manhole cover. It could barely be heard over the din of the bullet storm, but wailed loudly whenever there was a lull in gunfire. Soldiers streamed in from all over the base toward the source of the alert. Jeeps skidded into the area, picking up plumes of dirt, soldiers pouring out of them. Some of the jeeps had mounted machine guns on them.

Outgunned, outnumbered Baxter though grimly. He held a pistol and carried a few magazines, but no one had even come in range. *Smart*, Baxter reflected. *Hoping we surrender. No one wants to be the first casualty*.

ROEBUCK and D'Angelo emerged from the space behind them. They got into cover too.

"Where's Ramona?!" D'Angelo yelled over the guns.

Baxter hadn't noticed her absence, overwhelmed as he was by the soldiers' show of force.

"Up there," ROEBUCK pointed.

Above them, about twenty feet high, Ramona floated in a swirling wind. An empty sphere surrounded her, one no bullets or debris could penetrate. Her eyes were blank. Only the whites were visible.

"I'm detecting electro-magnetic energies that are beyond the maximum scale of my instruments. Some of these energies...I can *feel* them, but I don't even know what to call them," ROEBUCK spoke in awe. "She's far more powerful than I imagined."

"We need to think of *some*thing," D'Angelo told them. "She won't be able to keep this up much longer."

"Way I see it," Baxter explained, "we can surrender, spend the rest of our lives trapped in this base at the mercy of Major Monk. Or we take ourselves out. One way trip off this mortal coil, if you catch my drift. "

"*Shakespeare?*" D'Angelo hissed in disbelief.

"Seemed appropriate," Baxter replied. "Everyone dies in the end, that kind of thing. Course, we can always write our own ending in blood and smoke."

"I'd always imagined myself going out in a blaze of glory," ROBUCK mused. "Why make it easy on them?"

With these words, the bot stepped out from cover and began firing his Gatling in the direction of their enemies. An approaching jeep skidded hard to evade his fire, but turned over on itself, spinning on its roll-bars and throwing the driver and passenger out into the dust. Baxter's pistol made sure neither one got back up.

"D'Angelo, ROEBUCK, help me get it upright!" Baxter yelled.

He and the others rushed toward the wreck, but when they were halfway to it, D'Angelo called, "Incoming!" A rocket-propelled grenade zoomed toward them, trailing a spiraling cloud of smoke behind it.

With eyes wide and jaws slack, they turned and ran from the jeep. The rocket struck the fallen vehicle, and the concussive force of the explosion blew shards of broken machinery toward them. Ramona extended her field of impenetrability, and directed an angry burst of energy outward. A wave of force collided with the soldiers, and they were knocked onto their feet, momentarily stunned. Ramona's own energies were spent. She lowered herself to the ground, and collapsed in exhaustion once her feet touched the dirt.

D'Angelo picked herself up and took a look around. She knelt down next to Ramona and examined her. Once she was sure the girl was merely unconscious and not hurt in any way, she told Baxter and ROEBUCK, "She bought us some time, but now we need to make the most of it."

ROEBUCK scanned their surroundings, looking for an escape route. The area of the base they had emerged into was some kind of vehicle yard. Dozens of army jeeps were lined in front of a chain linked fence, topped with barbed wire. Some were covered in gray canvas, rippling in the wind, coated with brown dirt and dust. Larger vehicles, including tanks and Humvees, were scattered throughout the yard, in various states of assembly and repair. ROEBUCK eyed one of the Humvees closest to them, beneath a tall concrete observation tower that appeared mercifully abandoned.

"Follow me!" he yelled, and led his companions out of their cover toward his destination. He fired his Gatling at the soldiers across the yard, who were beginning to pick themselves up from the psychic blast Ramona had sent their way. They ducked back into cover, hiding behind a concrete barricade near a guard shack that protected one of the gates into the yard. Baxter and D'Angelo hurried behind the bot, carrying Ramona between them. The girl was still unconscious, her feet dragging twin tracks behind her. After a few hurried moments, they'd reached the Humvee.

ROEBUCK realized its door was locked, so he ripped it from its hinges, casting it aside with a clattering crash. He took off the panel from beneath its ignition, and examined its wires, connecting a pair that made the vehicle roar to life with a shuddering belch of smoke and exhaust.

"Help me get her inside," D'Angelo told Baxter. They brought Ramona inside the vehicle, propping her against the passenger side door. D'Angelo followed her in, and brought out some smelling salts from one of her lab coat pockets in an attempt to wake the girl.

"Looks like the hardware's still in fighting shape," Baxter said to ROEBUCK, eyeing the mounted machine gun on the Humvee's rear. "I'm gonna get her locked and loaded." He pulled himself up onto the back of the vehicle and began loading a belt of bullets into the weapon, sliding back its lever to load a shell into the clip.

ROEBUCK cast a glance at Ramona, groaning from her rude awakening, as D'Angelo did her best to bring her back to awareness. He put the Humvee into gear, and pushed the pedal to the floor, kicking up a cloud of dust as its rear wheels spun for a moment before launching them forward.

Bullets pinged off the metal exterior as the soldiers on the other side of the yard began to fire at them. Baxter shot back with the mounted gun, struggling to keep the powerful weapon's barrel level as a steady stream of lead poured from its mouth. Most scattered for cover, clambering behind vehicles and crates, anything solid that would keep them from being torn to pieces by the hellish onslaught

Baxter unleashed. A few brave souls returned fire, crouched low to the ground, hoping to earn a promotion or cash in a long-lasting death-wish. The gun shook Baxter's shoulders like an eager uncle, rattling his teeth and forcing him to hold onto it with a death-grip to keep it from firing over the soldiers' heads. After nearly half a minute of ceaseless torrent, the barrel of the gun began to glow orange, and Baxter poured water from his canteen onto it, steam hissing like a fiery snake. He began to reload, struggling to keep from slipping on the hundreds of spent shell casings that rolled around the gunner's compartment. A bullet flew past his head, kissing him with its wind and whistling death.

Inside the Humvee, ROEBUCK steered toward the nearest gate at what he hoped would be escape velocity. He steered sharply into corners, around guard towers and anywhere else he hoped that the vehicle would have any chance to avoid the soldiers firing at them. In the backseat, D'Angelo crouched low beneath the windows, and held on to Ramona, doing her very best to hold the girl upright, and to keep her awake and alert after the intense psychic energy she'd expended helping her companions escape the tunnels underneath the base. With every tight turn, they slid into the doors at each end.

They approached the gate of the compound at full speed. A pair of soldiers abandoned their defensive positions, which happened to be on the Humvee's path of destruction, and looked above them as a shadow blocked the sun. ROEBUCK followed their gaze, and the Humvee skidded to a halt.

Above them, an enormous metal frame loomed, with the same general shape of a human: four limbs, a torso, and a head. That's where the similarities ended. Propelling the massive machine in the air, the flame and smoke of rockets burned out of exhaust ports beneath its feet and from its back, blowing clouds of smoke and debris outward. One of its hands ended in a pincer-like claw, painted in yellow and black caution stripes. The other hand ended in a funnel, and if the small flame that glowed within was any indication, was some kind of massive blow torch.

The great hulking mass ended its descent with a clattering thud. ROEBUCK could hear the hydraulics of its limbs whine as it lurched forward. He put the Humvee in reverse and backed up a few paces, hoping to escape the range of whatever weaponry the hulking mass contained.

"Stop, or I'll fire!" a loudspeaker from the great heap demanded.

"Major Monk!" D'Angelo exclaimed, recognizing his voice. "And the OMEGA device. Looks like he finished the prototype…"

"What is it, Doc?" Baxter hollered above the rumble of the Humvee's engine.

"It's an Exo-Skeletal Battle-Suit," D'Angelo turned around and told him. "Adapted from a manufacturing and construction model. No obvious weak points."

"I'll do my best to evade it," ROEBUCK said, "and find another escape route."

"No," Ramona told him. "Bring us in close. Once I'm in range, I can reach into his mind. Control the OMEGA device from the inside out."

"Now, I don't think that's too—" Baxter's words vanished in a peel of rubber as ROEBUCK floored the accelerator, and the Humvee's tires spun in the dirt, hurling them toward Major Monk as fast as their vehicle could take them. "Damn it, ROEBUCK!" Baxter swore, nearly losing his grip on the gun turret and falling from his perch.

Instead, he fired his gun a few times, as a distraction and warning against any soldiers who had it in minds to poke their heads out and fire any pot shots. Most ducked back into cover, ready to defer to Major Monk and his OMEGA device until they received direct orders.

Monk grit his teeth, and looked out through the targeting ocular that covered his left eye, locking his reticle on the growing target of the HUMVEE as it came closer and closer. He hated to waste so many resources, *But I'll be damned if they slip out of here again*, he vowed, and launched a volley of missiles from a mounted shoulder turret. Their smoke streaked in spirals as they hurtled toward their target.

ROEBUCK saw the missiles launch and calculated their trajectory. He formed only one possible surviving maneuver. "Hang on!" he called loudly to his companions, as he hit his break and cut the steering wheel all the way to its left. The HUMVEE tilted in a screech of tires and a wave of dirt, two of its wheels coming slightly off the ground. For D'Angelo, time slowed as Ramona slammed into her, and the sun shined on some bullets shells that had fallen into the cab, dazzling her eyes in rays of brilliance. All four tires fell back to the surface, and as the HUMVEE rocked with the force of their weight, bouncing on its shocks, time snapped back into focus. They had spun three hundred sixty degrees, still heading in the same direction they'd been going, the missiles exploding harmlessly behind them.

"Cutting it a little close, don't ya think?" Baxter critiqued.

"Irrelevant," was ROEBUCK's reply.

He corrected the HUMVEE's course, and turned sharply, taking them behind the OMEGA device. Major Monk activated his craft's rocket thrusters, and lifted himself back into the air, rotating to follow the vehicle, but by then it was too late.

Ramona had slid the tendrils of her consciousness into his mind, and was controlling him now as a puppeteer guides a marionette. She raised the OMEGA's weapons systems into the air and launched all the ordinance that still remained. Bullets, missiles, rockets and grenades flew out from it, spewing flames and weaponry like an erupting volcano. The remaining soldiers broke and ran for cover, getting as far away from the OMEGA device and the Humvee as they possibly could.

An inferno erupted from the explosives, and when the ordinance came in contact with the vehicles, munitions and equipment in the base surrounding them, the calamity began to cascade. A chain reaction had started, one that made Baxter nervous. If a random shell or bomb struck their Humvee, it would be the end for all of them.

Eventually, the OMEGA had emptied its weapons completely. Ramona slumped over, drained once more by her exertion. Baxter saw no more soldiers nearby, so he hopped off the Humvee and made his way toward Monk.

The man looked panicked, and tried to lock himself inside, but Baxter was able to break one of the latches with the butt of his gun and pry the canopy open.

"Don't shoot!" Major Monk told him. "I'm the only chance you have of getting out of here alive."

"Exactly," Baxter said, "that's why you're coming with us."

He brought Monk up with him to the gunner's turret on the rear of the Humvee and held his pistol to the back of the major's head. "There's no reason you need to die either. Help us leave the base, and we'll let you go. If you try to lead us into some kind of trap, you'll be dead before it's sprung."

Monk grit his teeth. "Understood. This gate nearby, the one ROEBUCK tried to leave through before I intercepted you. It's still your best chance."

ROEBUCK overheard the conversation, and they sped out of the base and back out into the desert. It was twilight, and the sun was setting behind them. Ahead, the sky was dim, but when Baxter looked past the base, a pink sunset glowed through the smoke and cast long shadows on the sands.

"Do you still have our bikes?" Baxter asked.

"They've been disassembled," Monk explained. "You won't be getting them back."

"Damn it," Baxter cursed. He stewed in silence for a few minutes as ROEBUCK drove on. The bot headed back toward Baxter's home, the town full of ethanol refineries known as Whiskey, the one they'd left only a few days ago to help escort a convoy to Rock Springs. *So much has happened since then*, Baxter realized.

Once it became obvious no pursuers had followed them from the base, Baxter told ROEBUCK to stop the Humvee. ROEBUCK slowed to a halt, turned off the headlights and shut the engine. Through the rear window, Baxter saw Ramona's head slumped against Doctor D'Angelo still, asleep. She must have sensed they'd stop, because in another moment, Ramona's head came up and she yawned sleepily.

"Everyone out of the vehicle," Baxter announced. "We need to clear some things up."

The rest of his companions came out of the car, Ramona leaning against the doctor. They all turned toward Monk who appeared stoic, eyes narrowed and mouth flat. Only his white knuckles betrayed him.

"Lighten up, Major, we ain't gonna shoot you," Baxter said, "even though that would be the smartest thing to do. Just ain't my style to kill a beaten opponent."

"What are you gonna do with me then?" Monk asked.

"Let you walk back. Hope you make it to base before anything bad happens. But we have some questions first. ROEBUCK?"

"Where did your army find me?" ROEBUCK asked.

Monk sighed. "That's classified. Even from me. But I've heard rumors. Some say Area 51. There's data we recovered from you stored at the base. Copies might exist elsewhere, but it doesn't matter, because we've never been able to decrypt it. I know you're very old. Everybody who found you died long ago. The oldest records go back to the twentieth century. That's all I know."

D'Angelo looked skeptical. "What's the reason for all the experiments going on in that base? ROEBUCK, Ramona, the OMEGA device. What's it all for?"

Monk laughed grimly. "I don't have enough men to clear the raiders from the desert, or take control of the towns nearby. I'd hoped if we could create some kind of super-weapon, the army might be able to take over, restore order."

"That's it?" D'Angelo asked. "Who gives your orders?"

"I've no idea," Monk told her. "I receive transmissions sometimes, and take in the young men who find the base or are left there. But there's no greater purpose, that I know of at least."

"We're not getting much out of him," ROEBUCK said. "What else do you want to know, Baxter?"

"I want your word," Baxter demanded, "even though I know it might not mean much. I want your word you won't come after us again. Me, ROEBUCK, the girl or the Doc."

Monk grit his teeth. "I'll consider you lost assets. But I can't guarantee other military won't pursue you."

"I know," Baxter told him. "Go back the way you came. If you hurry, you should be able to get back before it's too cold. Just follow the tire tracks."

He hopped back in the gunner's turret, D'Angelo and Ramona sitting together in the backseat. The Humvee's engine rumbled as ROEBUCK touched the ignition wires, and they drove off into the night. Baxter watched the moon rise.

"What's that smell?" Ramona asked, her nose wrinkled in disgust.

"It's the distilleries," Baxter told her. "They turn crops into fuel. You'll get used to it."

"Ugh," Ramona said. "I don't want to."

Baxter grunted, and finished covering the Humvee with a tarp they'd found in its storage compartment. Despite Monk's assurance he wouldn't go after them, they didn't think it too wise to keep their stolen military hardware out in the open amongst so many prying eyes. ROEBUCK parked it about a half mile from the town, in the shadow of a small crevasse that kept it well hidden.

They walked from their hiding spot along a dusty trail through tents and tin shanties, the slums of Whiskey, rabble and refuse of the wastes. People scraping by however they could. Some of the small buildings were brothels, others housed dens of junkies, chasing their fix. A few were nomads and traders; most of the tents belonged to them.

Cook-fires were burning, filling the air with the scent of roasted meat. Baxter sniffed. *Armadillo. And rosemary?* A rumbling in his gut and a watering mouth confirmed what he already knew.

"I'm hungry," Ramona spoke.

"Me too, kid," Baxter told her. "C'mon, I think ol' Harley's shack is around here. He's usually got some grub to trade."

"A meal would do us all some good," D'Angelo agreed. "Give us some time to collect ourselves. And decide what to do next."

Harley's was a decent joint, among the best places in the slums one could go to fill their belly. You wouldn't know from looking at it. It was a tin heap, rusted and leaning like a drunk. Some lights glimmered from its windows, neon signs scavenged from bars and diners of old. Near the entrance, a German shepherd gnawed at an ostrich bone, and barked as Baxter approached. "Good to see you too, Sparky," he drawled as he rubbed the dog's head between its keen and pointed ears. He swept aside a canvas curtain that hung across the dive's entrance, and bid his companions to "Come on inside. I'll find us a seat."

A young women greeted them from behind a counter, giving ROEBUCK a not too subtle double-take. "Y'all sit anywhere you like. I'll be over in a sec."

They found a table in a corner booth, beneath a few more of those neon trinkets Harley had collected hanging from the wall. A vinyl bench wrapped its way around the table and sighed as the padding absorbed their collective weight. Paper menus, printed from a type-writer, rested on the table.

"What's good here?" D'Angelo asked.

"Whatever they got, it's good. Harley's an ace in the kitchen," Baxter told her. "He can make something tasty out of anything he finds. *Any*thing."

"That sounds a bit too inclusive for my taste," D'Angelo told him, "but I I suppose I can't be picky in our present circumstance. It does smell nice at least."

"Better in here than out there," Ramona remarked. "Possum *pie*? Barbaric. Don't worry, Sandy. I won't them turn you into anybody's lunch." Sandy poked her snout of a pack Ramona carried with her, and sniffed curiously, but the girl stroked the creature's snout, and the possum went back inside the bag and curled up, leaning on Ramona's hip as the bag rested on the diner's bench. Her pack had become the animal's new den of sorts. Mobile and cozy.

"Well, what do we have here?" a middle-aged man in a grease spattered apron came out from behind the diner's counter and looked over the occupants in his booth. "Baxter, and his crew of delinquents. When you didn't come back with the rest of Lester's convoy, we didn't know what the hell happened to you."

"Hey, Harley," Baxter returned the greeting. "Got caught up in a bit of mischief. Pulled our asses out of the frying pan, but don't got much to show for it."

"Ain't that the truth," Harley agreed. "Tell you what, my man, I'm feeling generous today. I'll trade ya that military uniform you're wearing for a damn feast. Gotta contact in town; think I could fence it for some dough."

"Well, that's a mighty generous offer," Baxter told him, "but if you take the clothes off my back, I ain't got much to change into. My old threads made their way through a mighty damn mess. Might stink to high heaven with what they been through."

"Eh, that's okay. We can wash 'em up in my sink tonight after I do the dishes. And I got some old rags you can throw on. Deal?" Harley asked.

"Deal," Baxter told him, "but it better be worth it. And no possum. Little lady's got a delicate appetite."

"Can do," Harley told him with a wink, and headed back into the kitchen. "Lucy!" he yelled as he made his way behind the counter. "Get these good folks some coffee and water. They look thirsty."

For a few minutes, the exhausted companions sipped their drinks and leaned back in their seats, glad for the respite. Days on the run, crawling through tunnels, riding across the wastes in the Humvee, and battling with Major Monk and his soldiers had all taken their toll. ROEBUCK looked fully recharged and alert from his time beneath the hot desert sun during their journey back to Whiskey, but Baxter, Ramona and D'Angelo still looked a little worse for wear.

The Doc rested her elbows on the table, and rubbed her eyes with the heels of her hands. A kaleidoscope of colors filled her vision, then faded as she blinked and sighed. "These flights across the desert and skulking around subterranean bases have ground me down. It's time for me to take some time to be a scientist again. To do a little bit of research. I'd like to perform some tests on Ramona, if she's willing. To see if we can discover the source of her abilities. Perhaps test their limits."

"Hmm," Ramona grumbled as plates of steaming ostrich meat, fried potatoes and cooked greens were placed by the servers onto the table in front of them. "I'm not sure I want to be somebody else's guinea pig. I had enough of that treatment under Major Monk."

"You'd have complete freedom, I assure you. I'll record data as you exercise your abilities." D'Angelo told her as she gripped Ramona's hand in her own. "And I'll help make sure nobody else is able to find us. I know you're used to taking care of yourself, but up here on the surface, things don't operate quite the same as they do down below."

"I'd take her up on the offer, kid," Baxter mumbled through a mouthful of biscuit. "The Doc can help you keep hidden from the authorities, and might be able to help you with your…gifts."

Ramona took a sip from her cup of tea, and blew a bit of steam from it. "It's a kind offer, but I'm used to being independent. It's a big, wide world out there, and I don't need a glorified babysitter to help see me through it. What do *you* think, ROEBUCK?"

ROEBUCK looked up at Ramona. His optic sensor flared red for a brief moment as he considered her inquiry. "Odds for survival do increase quite a bit among formed partnerships with complementary skills. For all your strength, it would be useful to have somebody guide you through this strange new world you've found yourself in. And I'm certain the doctor would appreciate your protection."

Ramona nodded and sighed quietly as she weighed her options. "Alright. I'll stick with you, Doc. As long as you realize we're partners. I'm nobody's apprentice."

Doctor D'Angelo grinned as she suppressed a chuckle. "Very well, then. We'll find a place in Whiskey where we can begin our studies. And where will the two of you be headed?"

Baxter and ROEBUCK exchanged a glance as they considered their options. Baxter cleared his throat and spoke, "Well ma'am, I suppose we ought to make our first bit of business getting a new pair of cycles. Hope to be able to trade that Humvee for a pretty penny, then hit the road. Not sure where to. Might have to see where it leads us."

"Yes," ROEBUCK agreed. "Best to keep all paths open to us for the time being."

With these words, the companions returned to their meals, all save ROEBUCK who analyzed Harley's table salt for trace impurities. The conversation settled around less serious topics, like the usefulness of possums and the price of ethanol. Their bellies grew full as the minutes passed. They grew languid, sated.

Baxter stretched his legs, and felt the itch of the road beneath his feet.

Acknowledgements

Thank you Matthew Kaufmann for encouraging me to write the story that evolved into this book's title piece. Thank you Lizzy Carraway and the other members of our writing group for providing helpful and constructive criticism for many of these stories. Thank you Sharon Scott, Rachel Short, Maple Needler, Young Kavi, Yoko Molotov, Jack Scally, Malon Kennedy Jr. and countless others in the Louisville literary and artistic communities for inspiring and supporting other young artists and writers. Thank you to all the writers, artists and musicians who are featured on American Fantastic for helping to build such a vibrant and varied artistic community.

And thank you Kelly Shiflet, who has thus far resisted the urge to murder me in my sleep. The love you give me is far more than I deserve.

Last, but not least, thank *you*, dear reader.

About the Author:

John Beechem is a writer from Louisville, Kentucky. He self-publishes on his website American Fantastic (**americanfantastic.com**), a community for writers and artists of all kinds. John has been published in the Cavalcade Literary Magazine , Tobacco Magazine and Sanitarium Magazine. He hosts the American Fantastic Radio Hour on ARTxFM (**soundcloud.com/john-beechem**), a community radio station, and has hosted Keep Louisville Literary, also on ARTxFM (**artxfm.com**).

His writing encompasses many pulp genres, including horror, fantasy, and science fiction. John also writes some poetry and literary fiction. He hopes to entertain his audience, to help them escape the reality of their day to day world, but also to inject higher themes and complex characters into his stories to create quality middle-brow writing. John is influenced by writers like George R.R. Martin, Margaret Atwood, and Octavia Butler, but also by video games, comic books, and other elements of pop culture.

If you would like to learn more about John or his website American Fantastic, you can follow American Fantastic on Facebook or e-mail John at **americanfantastic@gmail.com** .

John lives with his wife, Kelly, and their dog, Bella. He looks forward to the grand adventure that life has to offer them.

About the Artists:

Yoko Molotov is a multimedia artist specializing in transgressive, gender-fluid cartoons, comics, art books, poetry and video. She is also in the bands Sweatermeat, Tycoon Teens and performs solo as Harpy. She is currently pursuing a degree in fine arts. To commission work or contact Yoko, e-mail **yokomolotov@gmail.com**. You can find more of her work at **yokomolotov.net**.
[Back cover art, interior art page 15]

Jack Scally is an artist from Louisville, Kentuckyy. He most common mediums include watercolor, pens, acrylic paint, paint makers, charcoal, pastels, graphite, and oils. Most works are inspired from his fertile imagination, including places, scenery and works of fiction. His works can be found on Facebook (**Jack Scally Art)** and Instagram **@Eradelphic [Front cover art]**

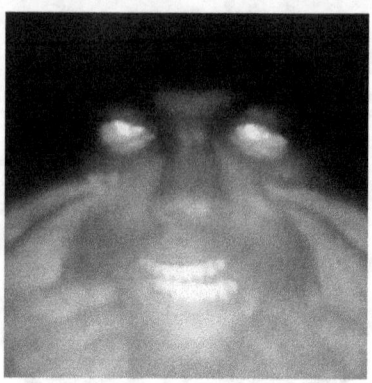

Malon Kennedy Jr. is a film-maker, visual artist and graphic designer from Louisville, Kentucky. He sketches, draws, and creates graphic designs personally and professionally. He has written and directed two films, **A Terrible Tale** and **Harbinger**. You can find Malon's films and other works on his website **jrmalonkennedy.com**. [Interior art page 12]

Delusions of Grandeur: Stories and Poems

These are a collection of marvelous, horrible, strange and compelling works. You are invited to ride on a wave of manic energy, as a young bi-polar man loses his grip on one reality and pierces the veil of another. Drive through the desert with a coyote, or human smuggler, until he unleashes the beast caged up inside him. Scavenge the wasteland of Brooklyn in the aftermath of a zombie apocalypse with a well-armed crew at your side. Witness the horror of a lynching, when Old Louisville was new, and learn the terrible price paid in a neighborhood that has earned its haunted reputation. Get to know a gunslinger and his robotic partner as they blaze through the American Southwest hundreds of years into the future, generations past the Great Fall.

Catch your breath with a bit of poetry. Or plunge into a narrative poem that tells its own story.

Feast your eyes on art and illustrations worth many thousands of words.

If you enjoy the pulp fiction of many genres, but still have a literary bone in your body, this is the collection for you.

When reality becomes a burden, enjoy a sojourn into the fantastic…

www.ingramcontent.com/pod-product-compliance
Lightning Source LLC
Chambersburg PA
CBHW071518170626
46811CB00007B/2894